PRISONER OF TERROR

PRISONER OF TERROR

MICHAEL JOHNSTONE

MADCAP

Published in Great Britain in 1997
by Madcap Books,
André Deutsch Ltd, 106 Great Russell Street, London WC1B 3LJ
André Deutsch is a subsidiary of VCI plc

A catalogue record for this book is available from the British Library

ISBN 0 233 99195 6

Printed in Great Britain

Hi! I'm Per. Per Dawson. Not the greatest first name in the world, but it's better than the one it's short for.

And wild horses wouldn't drag that from me.

I'm your average eleven year old. I try not to get into too much trouble - and usually manage it. But there have been the odd times when my parents and I haven't seen exactly eye to eye.

And I know if the policeman hot on my heels catches me and takes me home to Mum and Dad, this will be one of these times ...

CHAPTER

1

'Come back!'

I glanced over my shoulder and saw that PC Crosseye was hot on my trail.

PC Crosseye is not his real name. He's really Police Constable Patrick Crossman.

How do I know?

Well, apart from the fact that everyone knows everyone here in Avondale, it's not the first time that PC Crosseye and I have crossed swords.

Don't get me wrong. I'm not a candidate for the boot camp or wherever they send young offenders these days: it's just that sometimes our, and by our I mean the others in my gang, idea of fun and the rest of Avondale's don't match.

And when I said it wasn't the first time PC Crosseye and I had crossed swords it would have been more accurate to have said it was the third occasion.

Nothing serious. Just what Gran calls 'juvenile high spirits'.

The first was when they bulldozed the woods —

well, copse I suppose: OK the clump of straggly trees that we used to play in — at the edge of the field at the end of our road.

One day they were there. The next they were gone.

'Oh, didn't you know?' Mum had said when we'd trooped into the kitchen to tell her. 'They're going to build houses in the field.'

Houses? In our wood?

We didn't actually own it. But we looked upon it as our own.

We watched the workmen flatten bumps and dig foundations.

We watched them dump huge mountains of sand and piles of bricks.

And we hated them for it.

Where were we going to play now?

We really wanted to get our own back.

It was Keith Lumsden's idea.

We were sitting on his garden wall watching the builders pack up for the night. There was Keith, Colin Plenderleith, Franny Reid and Pam Brown.

'I wish there was some way we could stop them,' said Franny. 'I really miss those trees.'

'Or at least make some sort of protest,' said Pam, whose Mum and Dad were always going on marches to protest about things called Cuts.

Keith nudged me in the ribs. 'I know how we can protest,' he said.

'How?' Pam asked.

'Let's wait until they've gone,' Keith grinned. 'and there's no one else about.'

About an hour later, just as it was getting dark, and armed with as many spanners, wrenches and

2

screwdrivers as we could lay our hands on without being seen by our parents, we crept into the field.

●

Of course, we were number one suspects. But Crosseye and his merry men couldn't prove a thing. Or so we thought.

'Well if it wasn't you and your lot who took that cement mixer to bits and buried the parts all over the field, I don't know who it was,' he said, fixing his beady little eyes on me.

And as innocent as the altar boy Gran wanted me to be (she's got some odd ideas, has Gran) I'd stared straight back and said, 'Sorry, I can't help you, Constable Crosseye — sorry! Crossman!'

Everyone knew we'd done it and we would have got away with it if Colin hadn't still had a nut from the mixer when Crosseye asked him to empty his pockets in front of his parents.

We'd all been grounded for a month. Not, as Dad had said with the slightest hint of a twinkle in his eye, for taking the mixer to bits, but for lying to everyone about it!

The second time we'd crossed paths, Crosseye and I, was when he'd caught me cycling down the pedestrian precinct. Everyone else does it. But he'd picked on me, probably because of the cement mixer incident.

All I'd been doing was cycling. You'd have thought from the way he went on and on and on that I'd been caught trying to rob a bank or something.

And now he was hot on my heels, chasing me

down the path behind the row of houses I live in.

I don't know why I was running. Even if he didn't catch me, he knew very well who I was, and I'd been caught red-handed.

It was just after school one day in early October. Keith and Colin had been kept in for being cheeky to Pongo, our teacher. (Real name Mrs Black: but the perfume she wears stinks so much she pongs something awful, hence Pongo!)

We'd just had a test. Keith and Colin hadn't done brilliantly.

'Well, at least I got five right,' Keith had said when she handed out the papers.

'Five out of fifty is not what I call satisfactory,' Pongo had said. 'You and Colin Plenderleith had better pull your socks up!'

My two chums looked at each other, bent down and did exactly what she'd told them to do. Pulled their socks up!

We'd all thought it hysterical. Pongo hadn't.

Franny and Pam were on an outing with their class.

That's why I was alone that afternoon.

All the houses in our road have gardens at the back. Nothing grand. We've got a bit of grass, a flowerbed or two and a tiny vegetable patch in ours. And a couple of apple trees at the bottom.

You could count the apples that grow on them every year on the fingers of both hands and still have a pinkie or two to spare.

Now Granny Smith's apple tree is a different story.

It's huge, and every year the branches are weighed down with plump red apples, each one juicier looking than the one next to it.

She watches them like a hawk. Not surprising. It's easy to get into the path behind our houses and Granny Smith's apple tree is always being raided.

Not by me and the others.

We don't go out of our way to get into trouble.

But I was bored.

Mum and Dad were both at work.

Cass, my big sister, wasn't home from school yet.

I wandered out into the back garden and looked at the miserable offerings on Dad's trees.

Two doors down I could see the beauties on Granny Smith's.

'Don't be an idiot,' I said to myself.

But it was no good.

'OK. Be an idiot!'

I climbed over the wall and, ducking down to keep my head out of sight, crept down to Granny Smith's.

'I'll be in and out in in a flash,' I thought. 'She'll never see me.'

I would have been too, if I hadn't seen the juiciest, ripest apple I'd ever set eyes on.

And where was it?

Within easy reach?

No! As luck would have it, it was right at the top.

And as luck would have it, guess who'd just called on Granny Smith, to give her some bumf about setting up Neighbourhood Watch in our road, I found out later?

PC Crosseye.

(Not that we need Neighbourhood Watch in our

road. Granny Smith has been doing it on her own for as long as anyone can remember.)

I was halfway up the tree when I heard him shout so loudly he drowned out the whirring sound that announced the church clock was getting ready to strike four.

I looked down and saw him race up the garden path.

Quick as I could, I shinned to the end of a thick branch overhanging the lane and dropped down.

No sooner had I landed than I saw Crosseye squatting on top of the wall ready to pounce.

I flew down the lane.

'Per Dawson, you come back here!' he panted.

I glanced round to see how far behind me he was.

If I hadn't, I would have seen the person blocking my way in time to avoid crashing into him.

'Aaagh!' I screamed as I slammed straight into him.

Winded, I fell to the ground, gasping for breath.

There were stars dancing before my eyes.

Next thing I knew I felt myself floating upwards, and there was a curious, high-pitched voice in my ears. The only word I could make out was something that sounded like Loki. The rest could have been Double Dutch for all I knew.

CHAPTER

2

Slowly the stars started to fade.

I shook my head and looked around me, expecting to feel PC Crosseye's hand on my shoulder and hear him say, 'Got you!'

There was something on my shoulder all right.

But it wasn't Crosseye's hand.

When I realized what it was, I began to wish it had been.

It was a claw. Four enormous talons were digging into my shoulder so hard that I was sure they must be cutting into me.

And I wasn't in the lane behind my house.

For a moment I thought I was in a large cupboard with scarcely enough room for me and whatever was clutching onto my shoulder.

I squirmed, trying to wriggle free, but as soon as I moved, a second claw shot onto my other shoulder.

From the way it was angled, I realized there

must be two creatures behind me.

One of them said something. The words didn't so much fall on deaf ears as on ears that had no idea of what they meant.

Slowly I moved my head a little and tried to see what had me in their clutches.

The claws were at the end of plump little wrists dotted here and there with feathers, like a budgie with a bad case of the moult.

Another flow of verbal gobbledygook and another painful jab in the shoulder.

'Sorry!' I gulped. 'Just looking!'

I stood there in silence, but not for long.

There was a sharp click followed by what sounded like a key turning in a lock. A second later, the wall in front of me swung open.

'Come on,' I said to myself. 'You've been knocked out. You're dreaming. Time to wake up now!'

I closed my eyes and opened them again.

I pinched my thigh.

Nope! I wasn't dreaming, or whatever the verb for having a nightmare is. Nightmaring?

Standing in line in front of me were four of the most curious creatures I had ever seen. And judging from their claws and fluffily feathered arms, they were the same as the things behind me.

They were about two metres tall with brightly coloured bodies. They wore grey feathered cloaks almost reaching the ground.

Almost but not quite. The feet sticking out underneath reminded me of something. For a moment I couldn't think what. Then it came to me.

It looked as if they had legs and feet like a T-

Rex: that huge dinosaur that lived millions of years ago.

I looked up half-expecting to see great reptilian jaws agape, ready to gobble me up.

They had jaws all right. The jaws and head of an alligator.

What would you call something with dinosaur feet, a bird's body and an alligator's head? I asked myself.

I almost laughed for it was like one of those jokes you tell in the playground.

You know the kind. What would you call a man with a stone on his head? Cliff. That sort of thing.

Only this was no joke.

What *would* you call something with dinosaur feet, a bird's body and an alligator's head?

As two of them moved to one side and two to the other, I felt the claws dig deeper into my shoulder, urging me forward.

'OK! OK!' I cried. 'Not so hard!'

With four creatures in front and two behind, I was escorted along a brightly lit corridor until our way was barred by a stout wooden door.

The leading creature reached under its cape and pulled out a hefty wooden club.

Clutching it in its claws, it banged three times on the door.

On the third knock, the door swung open.

My four feathered friends in front stood to one side and once again I felt the claws dig deeper into my shoulders, urging me forward.

No sooner had I stepped through the door than it slammed shut behind me.

For a moment there was absolute silence, and

then the stillness was shattered by excited grunts and squeaks, cluckings and chirrupings. It was like being in a zoo.

The wall with the closed door was behind me. I tried to move forward but I'd only taken two steps when I found I couldn't go any further.

Groping all around me, I realized I was entombed in a glass shell. I felt like a battery in a bubble pack.

Beyond my see-through prison, on either side of the room in front of me, were two galleries crammed with creatures just like the ones who had taken me prisoner.

Some were bigger than others, some fatter. Some had jaws that were more pointed, others eyes that were smaller and ears that were larger, but they all came from similar moulds and they all wore grey, feathered capes.

There were another three of the beastly looking creatures facing me, seated on high-backed wooden chairs on a raised dais at the end of the room.

Their bright scarlet capes distinguished them from the rest. That and the small gold crowns perched between their ears.

A fourth, clutching what looked like a quill and wearing a smaller, silver circlet, was seated at a table between me and the other three.

Getting to its feet, it picked up a small hammer in its free claw and banged it on the table.

The chattering stopped immediately.

'Wow!' I thought. 'Old Frostface, our head, could do with one of those when he's trying to shut us up at weekly assembly on Friday mornings.'

The creature peered at me with his beady little

red eyes, dropped the hammer and picked up a sheaf of papers.

Slowly it began to walk towards me.

I saw its jaws move, but the only word I could make out in the mumbo jumbo filling my glass cell was the word I'd heard a minute or two before: Lok.

'Look,' I said, raising my hand to try to stop it in mid-flow. 'I think there's been some sort of mistake.'

It ignored me and carried on, sounding like a cassette on fast forward.

'Don't understand a word you're saying,' I said, not knowing if my words could be heard beyond the walls of my cell, but hoping that if I could hear it, it could hear me.

If what goes up must come down, then what goes one way must go the other, I hoped.

'Why are you talk-ing in Engl-ish?'

The voice was unlike any I'd heard before. It was high-pitched, very clear and had absolutely no expression at all. Each syllable was sharply distinct from the next, just like I'd always imagined a robot talking English would sound.

'Because I am English,' I said. 'Well, British. Dad's Welsh and Mum's got a Scots grandmother.'

'Lok-i,' the voice said. 'You're Jam-shid, like the rest of us.' It was like listening to a slot machine paying out several coins one by one. Still, at least I knew what they were, these alien creatures. Jamshids.

'No, I'm not a Jamshid,' I protested. 'I'm a human being.'

I racked my brains, desperate to remember

something I'd seen on a CD Rom at school. 'Human! From Earth! er, homo sapiens,' I cried in triumph.

'Lok-i. This char-ade is do-ing you no good. No good what-so-ev-er!'

'Charade? What's a charade?'

'A game pe-ople play!'

One thing I knew. This was no game.

Once again I closed my eyes and pinched myself, hoping that when I opened them again I'd be in PC Crosseye's clutches.

I was still in my cell.

By this time, the Jamshid was just on the other side of my cage.

When it opened its mouth, I saw two rows of teeth that seemed a little bit too large for my liking. And its mouth looked as if it was lined with shiny, soft, pink silk.

Suddenly a deep gurgling sound came from the far end of the room, like a whale clearing its throat. I looked beyond the nearest Jamshid and saw one of the red-cloaked variety open its jaws wide and fiddle with a back tooth with one of its claws.

'Must have had something stuck there,' I thought, shaking my head and shrugging my shoulders as another flood of Jamshid hit my ears.

'Sorry,' I said. 'I don't understand a word you're saying.'

'Hum-our him, Jan-nes,' said the red-cloaked Jamshid. 'Per-haps in ass-um-ing hu-man form, his brain has been aff-ect-ed in some way we do not un-der-stand.'

'Ver-y well,' said Jannes, staring at me.

I tried to look away, but his gaze held my eyes

as if I was being hypnotized.

'The pris-o-ner is charged with es-cap-ing from cust-od-y while a-wait-ing trans-por-ta-tion to the pe-nal is-land where he was sen-ten-ced to ten clos-ters ...'

'Closters?' I interrupted.

'Ten years ... hard la-bour.' As he spoke, he turned his back to me. 'Hav-ing been found guilt-y of trea-son.'

Suddenly he spun round, his claw pointing straight at me.

'I de-mand that the trait-or's sen-tence be doub-led!'

I did a quick count in my head.

Unless I got out of here, I was going to be nearly Dad's age before I got back to the Earth.

If I ever did!

CHAPTER

3

'Ladies and gentlemen of the jury,' the Jamshid went on (at least my ears seemed to be getting used to his curious way of talking), 'I will speak in English as suggested. This is an open-and-shut case.

'The prisoner, Loki ...'

'Per,' I tried to remind him. 'Per Dawson.'

I may as well have saved my breath.

'...slipped his guard,' he carried on, ignoring my interruption. 'And before his escape was noticed, managed to break into the transportation chamber where he beamed himself onto the planet Earth in the Solar System, Kyria.'

If I hadn't been so scared, I would have been quite interested.

'While on Earth Loki assumed the form and identity of the inhabitant you see before you.'

'Let me wake up. Now!' I screamed.

Jannes sprang round. 'A good performance,

Loki. But not good enough. Your escape was noticed almost immediately and we had you in our tracers the moment you arrived on Earth. And as soon as we could, we locked our relocator rays onto you and beamed you home.'

Jannes turned back to the galleries.

'The case for the prosecution is watertight. It has no flaws.'

Waving a piece of paper in the air, he said, 'You already have copies of the relevant print-outs. Do you find the prisoner guilty or not guilty?'

My hands flew to my ears to muffle the cries of guilty that filled my little prison.

A thunderous crack silenced them.

I looked up.

The three scarlet-cloaked Jamshids facing me rose to their feet.

'Loki, it is the sentence of this court that you serve a further five closters on the penal island in the Underworld. Take him away.'

A rush of air told me that the door behind me had been opened.

The two massive claws digging into my shoulders showed me there was no escape.

❂

'Listen!' My voice echoed round my ears. 'I really am Per Dawson. I think the Jamshid you're looking for must have been the one I banged into just before I arrived here.'

The three Jamshids fixed me with their beady little eyes and said nothing.

'Yes! That's it!' I cried. 'You had him in your

thingumyjiggs and just a split second before you pressed the button or whatever you do, we'd bumped into each other and I was where you thought *he* was.'

'Take him away!' the senior Jamshid said again.

'No!' I was pleading now. Well, wouldn't you be? 'You've got to listen.'

But it was no good.

The claws pulled me out of the court and back into the corridor.

This time I wasn't escorted. The Jamshids at either side dug their claws into my upper arms and dragged me along the passage so fast that I couldn't keep up with them and my feet scuffed along the ground behind me.

'Not so rough,' I shouted. 'I'm not likely to try to go anywhere, am I?'

I may as well have been talking to a brick wall.

When we came to a door, one of the Jamshids leaned forward and jerked it open. I was bundled through like a sack of potatoes.

The door banged shut behind me.

Now, I don't know about you, but I've never been afraid of the dark before, no matter how thick and black it may have seemed.

But I'd never been in such dense darkness before.

And I'd never been been in another solar system before. The fact that it was a first for the human race was no consolation.

Was I scared?

In a word, yes!

My mouth felt as dry as the Sahara Desert.

My knees were knocking so much I was surprised the bones weren't chipping away.

And I was shaking like jelly at a kid's birthday party.

Reaching forward like a sleepwalker, I felt my fingertips hit the door a few feet in front of me.

I ran my hand to the right until I found a wall and inched towards it until my way was blocked.

I felt my way back to the left until again I could go no further.

Whatever I was in was about two or three metres across.

A few seconds later I'd found out it was about the same from front to back.

Next moment, I thought I was about to leave my lunch behind me, for the floor sank beneath my feet and I realized I was in the fastest lift I'd ever been in in my life.

I plummeted down and down so quickly I was sure my ears were about to burst. I squeezed my nostrils together, swallowed hard and with a soft plop, they were clear again.

If I'd thought I was about to lose my lunch when the lift had started going down, I now thought I would swallow my teeth as we came to a halt so suddenly there was no way I could stop myself falling over.

No sooner had I landed than the door slid open.

Looking up, I saw a Jamshid peer into the lift.

'Loki?' he called. And then lapsed into Jamshidese.

'I'm down here, and I'm not Loki,' I said.

'Oh, yes!' At least he was speaking in English. 'It says here you're pretending to be — now where are my spectacles?'

Standing up, I saw him fumble in the pocket of his moulting old tunic and bring out the oddest glasses I've ever seen in my life. They were like a pair of earphones, only with glass lenses where the earpieces should be.

He fitted them over his head and glanced at the papers he was holding.

'Per Dawson,' I said. 'And I'm not pretending to be Per Dawson. I *am* Per Dawson.'

'Oh, Loki! Loki! Loki!' he tutted. 'Just 'cos you've nicked an Earthly body, you can't fool me. I can tell a Jamshid just by smelling him.'

'Smell away!' I said, pulling myself up to my full four feet ten inches. 'Go on! Be my guest!'

It's difficult to stand still when you're being sniffed by an alligator. Its scaly snout ran all over my body, sniffing here, sniffing there.

'Ugh!' He drew his snout away as if someone had just farted which, if the truth be told, someone almost had. 'Disgusting!'

'Convinced?' I said. 'That I'm not a Jamshid?

'Not like any Jamshid I've ever smelled before, I must admit. Maybe you are telling the truth after all.'

'So? What are you going to do about it?'

'What can I do about it? I can't send you back up. More than my job's worth. They're expecting another forty prisoners on the penal island. And Loki or not, you're going to be one of them.'

CHAPTER

4

'Why can't you send me back up?' I was getting desperate.

'That's the only lift that comes down here. And it won't go back up if there's anything in it. '

'Well, how do people, I mean Jamshids, get back up after they leave the penal island? How do *you* get back up from the Underworld?'

'Oh, I'll never go back up. No one who's sent to the Underworld is ever allowed back up there.' He jerked his head upwards. 'Once we've served our sentence, we're given jobs down here, or somewhere in the Lower World.'

My head started to spin. If no one was ever allowed back 'up there', how was I ever going to get home?

'There must be something you can do!' I was pleading again. 'Some way you can get back up and tell them that you know who I really am.'

'They're hardly likely to believe Old Amthest

now, are they? Not after what I did.'

'What did you do?' I was stalling for time.

'It's a very long story.' Amthest shook his head. 'Too long to go into now. Come on. Time to go. You're holding everyone else up. Not that they're all that keen to go, of course!'

I thought about running into the corridor beyond the lift and trying to escape. I might not know where I was going, but surely that was better than being shipped to some prison island, goodness knows where?

But just as I'd made up my mind to dart past Old Amthest, he reached into the lift and gripped my arm with his talons.

'Now, don't try to struggle,' he said. 'If you do, I'll have to get the Corems to help me and they can be very rough.'

The way the claw was cutting into my muscles was rough enough, thank you very much.

I let the old Jamshid pull me out of the lift and lead me along the passageway.

'Actually, it's not so bad, Gropium,' he said.

'Gropium!'

'The penal island,' he explained. 'Takes a bit of getting used to, but you're free to move around. There's no way of getting off, you see, only ...' His voice trailed off. 'The weather's not too bad, and the work's OK, depending on what you're given.'

'What did you do?' I asked. 'When you were there?'

'I was in one of the glince mines at first. Then they promoted me and eventually I was in charge of my own mine,' he said proudly.

'Look, Amthest.' I decided to have one last shot

at persuading him to let me go, for he seemed to be in a good mood.

'You know I'm not a Jamshid. Isn't there any way you can contact whoever you report to and tell them there's been a mix-up? Maybe they'll be so pleased with you that they'll let you go back up. As a reward for spotting a ...a ...' I was searching for a phrase I'd once heard Dad use, 'a miscarriage of justice.' The words came to me.

'No!'

So much for my powers of persuasion.

'Well, how about if I tried to help you escape. We could go back to my planet, maybe, and I'm sure you'd make a fortune in a circus or something. You'd be famous. You'd be the only Jamshid in the world. You'd be on the telly and maybe become a film star or something.'

'No!'

We stopped when we came to a heavy metal door.

Old Amthest let go of me and fumbled in his pockets again, mumbling, 'Where is it? What have I done with that key?' over and over again until at last he said, 'Oh, it's down there, is it? I'd forgotten that hole.'

'Should I make a run for it?' I asked myself.

'What's the point,' I answered my own question. 'I'd just be caught and probably sentenced to serve an even longer sentence.'

I saw the outline of Amthest's claws stretch into the hem of his tunic and a moment later he drew out a rusty old key.

The grating sound it made as he turned it in the lock was worse than chalk squeaking against a blackboard — you know how that sets your teeth on edge.

The door swung open.

Beyond it I could see a harbour. Tied to one of the bollards was a little sailing ship, the sort I'd seen in history books when we'd been doing the Ancient Greeks at school.

It was bobbing about on the greenest sea I'd ever seen. Greener than the grass in springtime. Greener than the greenest leaves on Granny Smith's apple tree.

'Blast that apple tree. If it hadn't been there, I wouldn't be here,' I said, aloud.

There must have been tears in my voice for Amthest turned to me and said, 'Look, Loki or whoever you are. There really is nothing I can do. If there was, well, I do believe I would try to help you.'

'OK, if you can't, isn't there someone who can? Anyone?'

Amthest looked away as if he was too embarrassed to look me straight in the eye.

'When you were talking about the island a moment ago you said there was no way of getting off, and then you said, "only". Only what? There is someone who knows how to escape, isn't there?'

Amthest looked around shiftily as if he was afraid of being overheard.

'When you get to the island, try to find Hymir. That's all I can say.'

'Hymir. What is it? A place? A man?'

Amthest's claw shot to his jaws. 'Sh!' he hissed. 'Someone may be listening. You never can tell here. Never can tell!'

'What is Hymir? Who is he?' I whispered.

'I can't say any more.' Amthest's voice was little more than a heavy breath.

Someone coughed so loudly right behind me that I almost jumped out of my skin.

I had been so intent on trying to make Amthest tell me more about Hymir, I hadn't heard anyone approach. My head shot round and I found myself staring into the gaping jaws of another Jamshid.

'Loki?' he said.

'Hang on a second, Loki,' Amthest said to me and turned to the other Jamshid and said something to him in the mumbo jumbo they called a language in this part of the Universe.

I recognized the words Earth, Kyria and English. I watched the Jamshid reach for a tooth at the back of his jaw, just like the Jamshid in the court had done. He rubbed it for a second then twisted it one way then the other two or three times.

'What's he doing?' I asked Amthest.

'I told him that Loki had taken on human form and that you only speak English. That's 47,320 in the automatic translator programme. In his mouth!'

When the Jamshid had finished fiddling with his tooth, he said, '*Qu'est-ce qui vous avez dire? Trois cents, vingt-et-un, oui?*'

'No, Vanor,' said Amthest. 'Three hundred and twenty.'

'*Excusez-moi,*' said Vanor and turned the tooth slightly.

'That's it,' he said. 'Come on now, Loki!'

'I'm not Loki, and he knows I'm not,' I cried.

Amthest shook his head.

'Now now, lad.' Vanor reached out and put a claw on my shoulder. 'The less trouble you give us, the less time you'll be on Gropium. You're the last one. Come on, now. Haven't got all day.'

He pulled me towards the ship.

A few minutes later, I was sitting on a damp wooden bench, my hands on a heavy oar.

'No wind today,' said Vanor. 'You lot'll have to row.'

I looked around me and counted.

There were forty of us. Thirty-nine villainous-looking Jamshids, and me, Per Dawson, about to set off for the prison island, who knew for how long?

CHAPTER

5

I'd only ever rowed once before. On the pond in the park at home.

To be honest, Dad had done most of the actual work, but he'd let me take an oar and hadn't been too angry when I sprayed him with water as soon as I dipped the oar in and pulled.

After a few goes, I'd soon got the hang of it and the oars had slipped through the water quite easily.

Rowing to Gropium was a different matter altogether.

For a start, there was no one in the rowing boat in the park banging a drum, shouting at us to row in time to the drumbeats.

And for seconds, the water in the pond hadn't been thicker than the pea soup Cass, my sister, had once brought home from school after one of her Home Economics classes.

'Try this,' she'd said. 'Mrs Walker said she'd never tasted anything like it.'

Neither had I.

It was as lumpy as porridge and tasted like a camel's armpits.

I don't know if what I was rowing through now had lumps in it or what it smelled like, but it was even thicker than the mess Cass called soup.

Every time I pulled the oar back towards me, I was covered in dollops of the stuff which clung to me like limpets.

After a few minutes I must have looked as if I had chickenpox with green spots instead of red ones.

Someone behind me growled.

'I speak English,' I said without turning round. 'It's 47,000 ... er ...' I racked my brains, '320 on your automatic translator thing.'

I waited a minute and asked him what he'd been trying to say to me.

'I said, watch it,' the Jamshid said gruffly. 'You're splattering me with the muck.'

'Sorry,' I gasped. 'It's just that I'm not used to it.'

'Quiet, Numbers 38 and 40,' boomed the drummer. 'No talking while you're rowing.'

'Don't snatch at the oars,' a muffled voice came from behind. 'Pull firmly and smoothly. And don't force them into the water. Let them sink in on their own.'

'Sink? In that muck? They'd have to be made of lead.'

'I said quiet!' the beater roared.

We rowed on in silence. The only sounds were the constant, repetitive drumming, the dipping of the oars into the sea and the laboured breathing coming from all around.

I could feel blisters begin to bubble up in my hands.

And every time I leaned forward and pulled back, I ached in places I never even knew I had before.

After about an hour, maybe a bit longer, the time between each drumbeat grew longer and longer.

Vanor appeared on deck for the first time and said something in Jamshid.

'What did he say?' I asked Number 40, my eyes still fixed straight ahead.

'He told us there's a wind rising from the west,' he said. 'We're going to raise the mainsail. We can stop rowing.'

'Thank goodness for that,' I panted, collapsing over my oar. 'I think I'm about to die.'

'Just as well the wind's got up. We're only about a quarter of the way there.'

I turned round and looked at the Jamshid behind me for the first time.

'So that's what they look like. On Earth,' he said, the little gurgling sounds he was making sounding like a baby laughing.

'What's so funny?' I asked.

'Well, I mean, look at you. Your eyes are far too close to each other. I shouldn't think you can even see halfway behind you, never mind all the way.'

I moved my eyeballs to the opposite ends of my eyes.

'See what I mean,' the Jamshid said. 'And call that a mouth? Couldn't eat enough to last for an hour through that.'

'At least I'm not fat,' I said, looking at the

Jamshid's great big bulging belly.

'Oh, that'll soon come off after a spell down the glince mines. The weight sweats off you down there.'

'You mean you've been to the island before?'

'Third time,' my companion said. 'Not that I'm guilty, mind.'

'Don't tell me. You were framed each time?'

The Jamshid nodded. 'Oh, I'm Clam, by the way. You're Loki, aren't you?'

'No,' I sighed for the umpteenth time that day. 'Loki's still on Earth. I was beamed up by mistake. My name's Per.'

'Likely story,' scoffed Clam. 'Tell that to the Three Wise Ones!'

'If they're the three with little gold crowns between their ears, I tried to, but they wouldn't believe me.'

'Didn't believe me either, when I told them I'd been framed.'

'If you've been to the island before, do you know who, or what Hymir is?'

'Hymir!' Clam gasped, blinking several times in succession. 'How you know about Hymir? You want to be careful, you do.'

'Why? What is it?'

Clam looked around him, just as Amthest had when he'd mentioned Hymir. But no one was paying any attention to us. They were all watching three small Jamshids climb up the mast to the yardarm.

'Ropes must be stuck again,' said Clam. 'Happened the last time I was being taken to the island.'

'Tell me about Hymir,' I urged him.

'Keep your voice down,' he said. 'Want to get us thrown overboard?'

'Sorry!'

'Hymir used to be a Wise One. But the other three thought he was getting too big for his boots. So they ganged up against him and had him charged with treason ...'

Suddenly he stopped and looked at me curiously. 'Anyway, why am I telling all this to you, Loki? Everyone knows what happened.'

I was getting so fed up saying I wasn't Loki that I shrugged my shoulders and said, 'I've forgotten. I think I must have banged my head or something when I was on the run on Earth.'

'I believe you, thousands wouldn't. Anyway, they claimed he'd been selling secrets to the Kunkernuckles, our enemies in case you've forgotten that too,' he said, winking at me knowingly.

'And had he?'

'What, Hymir? No way! Still, they made the charges stick and Hymir was sentenced to life imprisonment on Gropium. And when they say life they mean life.'

He looked puzzled for a second.

'Funny though,' he went on. 'They do say he's the only one who knows a way out and could get back up, if he wanted to. But he's biding his time, plotting his revenge, I wouldn't be surprised.'

'If he knew a way up,' I said. 'Do you suppose he'd know a way I could get back to Earth?'

'Come on, Loki.' Clam held his head to one side and stared at me. 'Who are you trying to kid?'

'OK,' I said. 'Just suppose I was telling the truth,

and I really was Per Dawson. From Earth. Would Hymir know a way I could get back?'

'Well, if anyone could, he could.'

Suddenly he smiled. 'Look,' he cried, pointing at something behind me. 'On the yardarm. It's an Alkanvaald!'

I spun round in my seat and looked up.

There, perched on the pole that was lashed horizontally to the mainmast was the biggest, meanest-looking bird I had ever seen.

'That's a good luck sign, if ever there was one.'

'Good luck?' I said. Even from where we were sitting, its bright, glaring eyes sent a shiver down my spine. 'It looks pretty nasty to me.'

'No!' said Clam. 'They're harmless cowards. Never attack, do Alkanvaald.'

'Are you sure?' I backed away a little, for I could have sworn it was staring right at me, and I didn't like the expression in its eyes.

CHAPTER

6

One minute it was staring at me, the next it was swooping down straight towards me.

'Look out!' Clam cried, knocking me to one side so hard that I fell off the bench and landed on my back on the wooden deck.

I felt a splinter pierce the back of my leg and winced with pain.

Worse, I was wallowing in what looked like green glue.

I looked to my right and saw green gunge oozing up between the planks.

'What the ...? I curled my nose up.

'Seepage!' said Clam. 'You always get a bit of seepage, especially in old wrecks like this.'

'Gee, thanks,' I retched, seeing another wave of the thick bile leak towards me.

I turned my head to get my mouth and nose out of the way, glanced up and saw the Alkanvaald circling in the air overhead.

'Never seen an Alkanvaald behave like that before,' said Clam, but even as he spoke there was a loud flapping and it shot downwards, dive-bombing straight for me again.

For a second I lay there mesmerized but then, just when its gleaming, black beak was about to pierce me in the shoulder, I managed to roll over under the bench.

I was now drenched in muck.

It was as if I had dived into a bath full of dirty green oil that clung to me, spreading all over my body, seeping into my hair, up my nose, under my fingernails.

'Get off!' I heard Clam yell. 'What's got into you?'

I peeked up from under my shelter and saw the bird flapping around his head, pecking wildly at his scaly skin.

Clam was doing his best to fend the thing off, but it was in such a frenzy it must have been like trying to keep a swarm of mosquitoes at bay.

The Jamshid's claws flashed through the air, occasionally hitting home, but more often than not slamming into his own shoulders.

With Clam's screams ringing in my ears, I managed to raise myself onto one arm, despite the thick green globules trying to pull me back.

I got to my knees, arched my back and with an almighty tug got to my feet.

The oar! If I could get the oar I might be able to beat the Alkanvaald away from Clam.

Heavy? I'd never tried to lift anything so heavy in my life before.

There was no way I could pull it into the boat,

never mind try to use it as a weapon.

'Get off!' Clam's shouts were becoming more and more desperate. 'Go and peck something your own size. Get off, you evil monster!'

I rubbed my hands across my bottom, to try to get rid of some of the muck.

But the stuff was so thick all over my bum that I ended up with even more of it on them.

As I pulled them away, my thumb caught in my belt.

My belt!

Quick as a flash I unbuckled it and began to whirl it round my head.

The blast of air around the tops of my legs reminded me that the jeans I'd been wearing were a new pair Mum had bought in the Sales.

'They're far too big,' I'd protested, clutching the top to keep them up.

'Never mind,' she had said. 'They were a bargain and you'll soon grow into them. Use a belt!'

I couldn't begin to imagine what she would have said if she could have seen me now, standing on the deck of the little ship in the middle of a sludgy green sea, swirling my belt above my head, trying to fight off a demented bird with one hand and desperately trying to stop my jeans from falling over my knees with the other.

Yes, I could! 'I hope those boxers are clean!' she would have shouted.

There was a very satisfying thud of leather against feather as my belt hit home so hard it fell from my hand.

With an anguished squawk and a loud flap of its enormous wings, the Alkanvaald soared into the sky.

'Where's my belt gone?' I yelped, putting both hands on my waist.

'Thanks,' said Clam, rubbing a claw up and down his snout. 'Never knew Alkanvaalds had such sharp ...' He broke off and pointed at me.

My jeans were round my ankles and my boxers were flapping in the wind.

'What on earth are those?' he asked.

'What?' I gulped. For I suddenly remembered that the only clean shorts I had been able to find that morning were a pair Cass had given me for Christmas. They were red, dotted here and there with Santa Claus and his reindeers riding through clouds of white snowflakes.

Before I could answer, I heard Clam shout, 'Look out! It's back!'

Too late!

I felt an excruciating pain shoot through my bottom as something sharp pierced one of Santa's sleighs — the one just above a leg hole.

I fell forward and was just about to crash into Clam when he dodged to one side.

For the second time in as many minutes I was floundering around in the sticky sludge slurping all over the deck. Only this time I had a bird biting my bum at the same time.

As I rolled over, I felt something soft flatten beneath me, and the pain got sharper and sharper as the Alkanvaald's beak sank deeper and deeper into my flesh.

Clam held out a claw for me to hold on to as I clambered to my feet.

I reached round and tugged the squashed, dead

bird free.

Its beak was stained with blood. My blood.

'What's going on here?' I recognized Vanor's voice.

'The Alkanvaald,' said Clam, pointing to the sorry-looking thing in my hands. 'It went berserk!'

'The Alkanvaald!' Vanor was obviously astonished. 'Never. You must have been been provoking it,' he said sternly. 'Even so, I've never known one turn nasty before!'

'Me? Provoke it?' Clam's voice was full of outraged innocence.

'What's that on its beak?' asked Vanor.

'My blood!' I said, rubbing my bum with my free hand. 'That thing went right through my boxers,' I went on. 'Probably ripped them to shreds at the back. Mum'll go spare when she sees them.'

When! I should have said if, but I wasn't really thinking.

'That's not blood!' said Vanor. 'Jamshids' blood's yellow. Turn round!'

'Can I pull my jeans up first?' I said, starting to feel a bit of a nerd at the way all the other Jamshids were now looking at me.

I don't usually mind being the centre of attention, but not when my bum was probably sticking through great holes in my boxers and my jeans were round my ankles.

I was annoyed too. Why had none of them tried to help Clam and me?

As I leaned over to pull them up, I heard Vanor say, 'That's funny. That looks like red blood.'

'Of course it's red,' I said. 'Human beings have red blood.'

'He's taken over human form, remember,' said Clam. 'That'll be why the blood's red.'

'No!' said Vanor. 'When a Jamshid takes over anything else's shape or body, it's only the outside that changes. Underneath he remains a Jamshid.'

He looked me up and down. 'Maybe he is telling the truth after all. I heard back at port that he claimed there was a mix-up when Loki was being beamed back up.'

I felt as if he was looking right through me. 'Maybe Loki is still on Earth and we've got an Earthingum on Jamshidia by mistake!'

'Yes!' I cried, punching the air with both fists, then clutching my jeans as they threatened to drop to the deck again.

'Could someone get me my belt, please?' I asked. 'It's down there!'

Clam reached into the green gruel and picked up my dripping belt.

'Thanks!' I said, taking it from him, and starting to loop it onto my jeans. 'So, if you now believe I really am Per Dawson, is there any way you can help me?'

Vanor shook his head.

'Knowing it's one thing. Doing something about it is quite another thing. Quite another thing!'

CHAPTER

7

'Well, he's no good to me,' said the Jamshid, running his eyes all over me. 'Look at him. He couldn't lift an empty glince pan, never mind a full one.'

'Hm!' Vanor rubbed his jaws with his right claw. 'See what you mean, Swingo. How about odd jobs in the maintenance yard?'

Swingo shook his head. 'Even that's probably too heavy for him. No! Sorry, Vanor. Tried the kitchens?'

'First thing I did. They're full.'

'Look!' I said. 'You've been dragging me round the island for days now. I'm too small for the glince mines. Too big for the Howgrod factory ...'

'Couldn't squeeze through the weftloom grids,' Vanor explained to Swingo.

'I'm too thin for this and too fat for that,' I went on. 'Why don't you just let me go?'

'We've been through all that,' said Vanor. 'You got ten closters. And ten closters it is!'

Ten closters! Ten years! I felt tears well up in my eyes.

'Loki!' I heard someone shout. 'Recovered from the Alkanvaald yet?'

I looked round and saw Clam at the back of a line of rough-looking Jamshids, heading for a cave in the cliffs nearby.

'Still a bit sore,' I shouted, waving at him and watching him disappear into the cave which I knew was the entrance to the glince mine.

'Look,' I said, wiping the tears from my eyes. 'You know I'm not a Jamshid. Can't you at least get a message to whoever you have to talk to? You must take your orders from somewhere. Someone!'

I saw Swingo and Vanor exchange glances.

'There is a way, isn't there?' I cried. 'You've got to tell me. Please.'

They both shook their heads.

'Listen, Loki ...'

'Per!'

'OK! Per. The only one that knows is ... is ...'

'Hymir!' I cried. 'Hymir knows a way, doesn't he?'

'I have heard,' said Swingo, coughing to clear his throat, 'that the Fallen One is not in the best of health and needs help.'

'But if it ever got back. Up there ...' whispered Vanor.

Swingo looked round to make sure no one else was within earshot.

'I wouldn't say anything. And if anyone notices he's gone, you could always say another

Alkanvaald got him. I heard what happened on the ship.'

The two Jamshids looked at one another for a moment.

'And I have heard that things are a bit - er - unsettled up there,' Swingo went on. 'Have been ever since ... ' his voice fell to little more than a whisper ...' Hymir was sent here. He's got his supporters, you know.'

Vanor nodded. 'And they are growing in number every day, if what I hear is correct.'

'Exactly!' said Swingo. 'So who knows what may happen. So maybe ...'

'If things do change and Hymir is recalled, it wouldn't do us any harm to be in his good books.'

'You mean I can go to Hymir?' I found I was whispering too.

'Can't actually take you there myself, you understand,' said Vanor. 'But I can point you in the right direction.'

✪

'Good luck, Per!' Vanor held out his claw. 'I mean that.'

'Thanks,' I said, taking the claw in my hand and shaking it firmly.

'Know where you're going?'

'I think so. Through the wood, taking each right-hand fork until I get to the Great Candlewick Tree, and then I start taking the left ones!'

'Right!'

'You said left.'

'I mean right: as in correct.'

'Oh! Right!'

'Make sure you take the forks just as I've told you. If you don't you'll be in trouble.'

'I'll remember,' I said.

'Good. 'Bye then.'

'Goodbye!'

A few minutes later I was in the wood. The trees were so tall I couldn't see the tops of any of them, and their trunks were thicker than any trees I'd ever seen before.

Underfoot, grass as yellow as corn was dotted with great red blooms swaying from side to side. When they moved it was like looking at cherries slurping around in custard.

Each right-hand fork I took led me deeper and deeper into the wood. The trees started to grow closer together, in places so close that it would have been impossible for even someone as small as me to squeeze between them.

Sometimes, the yellow grass gave way to dense undergrowth — stubby little bushes with lethal-looking spikes and twisting tendrils winding themselves round the trees.

Overhead, the tops of the trees appeared to meet and grow into each other, making the wood as gloomy as a damp November afternoon.

Vanor had warned me that it would be dark, but he'd said it was quite safe. 'No Alkanvaalds in there,' he'd grinned.

Even so, I half-expected something to jump out of the shadows at any minute and whisk me off to some underground lair. And if that happened, who would miss me? Vanor didn't expect to see me again, and Hymir didn't know I was coming. The thought wasn't exactly comforting. In fact, it was distinctly worrying!

After about an hour, I came to a tree that was much thicker than the rest.

'This must be it,' I said aloud. 'The Great Candlewick Tree.'

I stopped for a minute or two, then carried on, taking the fork to my left.

It got gloomier and gloomier and gloomier, and I started to feel more and more uneasy.

You know how it is when you're on a bus or walking along the street and you can feel someone looking at you even though you can't see them. And when you turn round, your eyes meet theirs for a fraction of a second before you both blink and turn your gaze away.

Well, that's how I felt now as I walked on.

I was sure I was being watched. And when I heard a twig snap some distance to my left, I was quite certain.

'Who's there?' I called.

Silly question. If someone or something is keeping a secret eye on you he, she or it is hardly likely to answer, are they?

'Keep calm,' I told myself. 'Vanor said there were no Alkanvaalds in here.'

But he didn't say what else there might be lurking among the trees.

I quickened my step.

Another twig cracked.

I heard leaves rustling first behind me and then to my left.

I lengthened my stride.

So did whatever was on my heels.

'Go away!' I shouted. 'Leave me alone!'

I dodged in and out of the trees as fast as I could.

I came to a fork in the path and shot round the tree in the middle.

It was only when I was past it that I suddenly thought I couldn't remember if I'd gone to the left or the right.

Vanor's words, 'If you don't, you'll be in trouble', echoed through my head.

'I'm in trouble anyway,' I thought.

My lungs felt as if they were about to burst.

I had to stop. I had to.

Just ahead, I saw a branch about an arm's length above my head.

I slowed down and stopped when I reached it.

Jumping up, I grabbed the branch in both hands and started to pull myself up.

Just in time, for even as my legs were still dangling a few feet above the ground, I felt something snapping at my ankles.

I swung my body forward and back.

There was a pained howl as my feet slammed into something.

With a great grunt, I pulled myself up and lay snake-like along the branch.

When I looked down, my heart almost missed a beat.

I was staring into the eyes of three hideous two-headed dogs! And the way their twelve eyes were looking straight into mine had me quaking all over.

CHAPTER

8

Arching its back, one of them sprang upwards.

Both its jaws were wide open, revealing great yellowish teeth that looked sharp enough to take a toe off given half a chance.

Clutching the branch so tightly that my hands started to go numb, I slithered along the branch towards the trunk a few feet away.

Another of the hideous hounds shot upwards and almost managed to snap at the branch.

I saw the third beast, bigger than the others by more than one of its heads bend its back legs, obviously getting ready to leap in my direction.

By now, the trunk was just within my reach. Using it to steady myself, I got to my feet and was standing on the branch just as the great animal leapt up at me.

I was so terrified, I almost lost my balance, but just when I thought I was going to topple over and end up as a dog's — sorry dogs' — dinner, I managed to right myself.

There was another branch just above me.

Stretching up to my full height I gripped it and started to pull myself up. For a moment I swung back and forward and then, using every remaining ounce of strength, I pulled myself up like one of the gymnasts I'd seen on television doing exercises on a set of bars.

I was well out of reach now, but that made no difference to the three terrifying beasts. One by one, they leapt up and down like three manic yo-yos on an invisible string.

The fact that I was safe for the moment was not much consolation, and I shuddered at the thought of losing my balance and plunging to the ground and six sets of snarling, gaping jaws getting ready to rip me apart.

'Please make them go away,' I prayed.

My prayer was answered — by three long, bloodcurdling howls.

So much for prayer!

Suddenly the dogs stopped and stood very still, their ears erect.

'Please make them go away,' I said again, giving prayer one more chance. 'Please!'

One of the hounds bared all its teeth and growled deeply. Then the three of them bounded back through the undergrowth.

'Thank you!' I gasped. If I ever got home alive I promised I would join in the hymn-singing at weekly assembly rather than look down at my feet, mouthing the words like everyone else.

And I wouldn't tell Gran to get knotted when she went on about how proud she'd be if I became an altar boy!

I don't know how long I stayed up that tree before I dared to climb down. Five minutes? Ten, maybe?

I do know that when I lowered myself to the first branch then jumped to the ground, I was shaking so badly that if I'd been holding a glass of milk it would have turned to butter in a flash.

My mind was racing as I tried to decide what to do. Vanor had said that if I stuck to his directions I'd be quite safe.

Being attacked by the hounds from you know where hardly counted as quite safe in my book. I must have gone wrong at the last fork.

'A branch,' I thought. 'Better get a branch or a stick of some sort, in case these beasts are still on the prowl.'

I saw one low enough for me to reach and thin enough, I hoped, for me to break off.

I pulled and pulled until, with a satisfying splintering sound, it came away from the trunk.

Pulling off the twigs and leaves sprouting from it, I made my way back to the last fork. As I approached it I saw the tree in the middle was to my right.

I had taken the wrong turning.

Keeping a wary eye all around me, I made my way down the path leading from the left-hand fork.

My heart leapt to my mouth several times when the breeze rustled through fallen leaves, making me think there was something on my trail again.

But when I looked round, there was nothing.

The trees started to thin out and soon I was

walking through open country. Not that it was at all like the countryside at home.

The grass was much sharper, now dangerously sharp, and was no longer yellow but pale blue.

Curious plants, almost but not quite like little cactuses, were growing everywhere.

Overhead the sky was overcast, a deep heavy purple.

Suddenly I noticed I was casting a shadow in front of me. I looked behind and saw the sky had cleared a little and a watery sun was starting to shine through.

After a time, I realized I was casting not one but two shadows.

'Gosh!' I gasped when I saw two suns in the sky, huge balls of orange moving slowly in opposite directions.

On and on I walked, sweating in the heat of the Underworld's two suns.

The ground began to get steeper and steeper and my legs started to ache as I toiled uphill.

Eventually I reached the top.

Panting, I fell to the grass trying to catch my breath.

The suns were burning down and my eyes were growing heavier and heavier ...

✪

I woke with a start.

'Where on Earth am I?' I said, sitting up.

Then I remembered I was nowhere on Earth! I was in the Underworld of another planet, in another solar system, looking for an alien who I hoped would help me get back to my own place and time.

I stood up and stretched, feeling refreshed after my snooze.

I was on the brow of a hill I had thought, but what I saw when I looked down made me catch my breath.

I was standing on the edge of an enormous crater filled with a blue lake that glittered in the suns.

Bobbing about in the wavelets lapping the edge, was a small rowing boat.

Vanor hadn't mentioned a boat, and I'd followed his directions exactly apart from one wrong turning which I'd put right.

Hoping for the best, I slid down the scree to the water's edge, took off my shoes and socks, rolled my jeans up and paddled to the boat.

The oars were lying on the bottom.

'Oh well,' I sighed, clambering in. 'Here we go rowing again!'

My hands were still blistered from my spell on the boat with Clam and the other Jamshids.

'Ouch!' I winced as the wooden oars chaffed the raw skin on the palms of my hands.

Rowing the boat across that lake was a lot easier than pulling at the oars of the prison ship.

Despite the pain in my hands, I started to enjoy the splashing of the oars and the regular pulling and pushing.

But as the far side came closer, I heard something that made me wish I'd stayed on the shore now far behind me.

A bloodcurdling barking I'd hoped never to hear again as long as I lived.

CHAPTER

9

The oars froze in my hands, and I sat quite still watching the three two-headed dogs — or their exact doubles — break through the undergrowth fringing the little beach I was nearing.

Their barking grew more frenzied as the tide carried me towards them.

Suddenly the suns caught something glinting in the water slopping around in the bottom of the boat: an anchor I hadn't noticed when I'd clambered aboard.

When I reached to pick it up, I found it was attached to a coil of rope.

At least I had a weapon if the ferocious beasts splashed through the water and attacked.

I pulled the oars in and stood up, desperately trying not to rock the little boat.

Throwing up a great shower of spray, the three monstrous dogs flung themselves into the water and started to swim towards me.

The boat swayed violently from side to side as I bent down to pick up the anchor.

I stumbled towards the prow, clutching it in both hands, and dropped it there.

Then, grabbing the anchor rope, I raised my right hand and began to whirl the anchor round and round above my head. There was a loud swishing sound as it cut through the air.

And when I moved my hand forward and brought it down a little, the anchor scythed through the water, then up round the back of my head before coming round and plunging into the water again.

The dogs separated. One was right in front of me, treading water just out of the anchor's reach as it skimmed the water a few feet from the hound's snarling jaws, sending up a shower of foam.

The second hound swam to the right and the third to the left.

I could keep one at bay, maybe two.

But three coming at me from different directions!

I swung the anchor first one way then another, rocking the boat violently from side to side so wildly that it was a struggle to keep myself upright.

I was soaked by the spray I was lashing up, and my arms were aching from the effort of swinging that anchor round and round, up and down.

I looked up. Great clouds were scudding across the sky. Suddenly they started to spin as I felt my balance going.

Next thing I knew I was thrashing about underwater.

I came up, gasping for breath, like a dolphin breaking the surface.

Now I've been swimming since I was six or seven, but splashing around in the local pool with my mates hadn't exactly prepared me for what I faced now.

I shot round in the water. Ahead, between me and the shore, one of the dogs was swimming towards me, both mouths agape.

The other two were nowhere to be seen.

I looked behind me.

There they were, cutting through the water like torpedoes honing in on a stricken submarine.

Taking the deepest breath ever, I dived underwater, my lungs pressing against my ribs like two bulging balloons.

Down and down I went and then, hoping I was heading in the right direction, I made for the shore.

My lungs were bursting: little flashes of light were dancing before my eyes, but just when I thought I was about to pass out, my feet hit the bottom.

My head broke through the surface and I found myself standing shoulder high in the water.

Wiping it from my eyes, I could see the shore about twenty, maybe thirty metres away.

No Olympic swimmer has flashed through water quicker than I did then.

My arms cut through the waves. My legs were thrashing so frantically I must have thrown up more spray than the Niagara Falls.

When I felt pebbles beneath my knees, I stood and ran for the shore as fast as I could.

The excited barking ringing in my ears told me

my nightmarish attackers were not far behind.

I sprinted along that beach, trying to ignore the sharp pebbles cutting through the soles of my shoes.

Desperately I looked around for a tree to climb, but there was nothing but dense stubby little bushes beyond the beach, growing so close together it would have been impossible for me to break through them. For a moment I thought it might be worth trying, but one look at the sharp leaves sprouting from them quickly changed my mind.

Anxious to know how far ahead of the three dogs I was, I jerked my head round just in time to see one of them leap through the air towards me.

Two great paws landed on my shoulders, sending me tumbling to the ground with such force every last ounce of air was knocked from my lungs.

Pebbles dug painfully into my stomach and chest as I gasped for breath.

I managed to roll onto my back.

Immediately, I wished I hadn't.

Twelve fiery eyes were staring down at me.

Six sets of jaws were wide open a few inches above me.

'Please,' I sent a silent prayer heavenward. 'Please let it be quick!'

I clamped my eyes shut and braced myself for the pain.

None came.

I heard their steady panting and felt their hot breath on my face.

'Come on!' I think I said it aloud. 'Get it over with!'

Still nothing.

I screwed my eyes up and opened them into little more than slits.

They were still staring down at me, still jutting menacingly from the sides of their many mouths. But they had been joined by something else.

A creature I recognized.

A Jamshid.

His great, alligator jaws moved.

'Tisiphone! Alecto! Magaera!' he grunted.

'What?' I said.

His beady little eyes looked at me.

He grunted again!

'Sorry,' I said. 'I don't understand.'

He looked puzzled and once more he grunted something.

I pointed at my chest. 'Me — speak — Eng-lish!' I said, jabbing myself with each syllable.

The Jamshid reached into his mouth and played with one of his back teeth.

'English?' he said. 'How does an English-speaking alien come to be here?'

'Alien!' I was about to protest. 'You're the alien,' I was going to say. But I stopped myself. I suppose that to him and everyone else on Jamshidia, it was me who was the alien!

'It's a long story.' I said, raising myself onto one elbow and squinting up at him. 'Are these your dogs?'

He nodded.

'Could you — sort of — call them off, if you know what I mean?' I asked in my politest voice.

'Call them off? They wouldn't harm a fly. Would you, girls?' He bent over and stroked one of them behind the ears.

'I don't know about flies,' I protested, 'but they were all set to get me. In the water, there,' I went on, pointing at the little boat that was still bobbing about in the water a few metres from the shore.

'And they chased me up a tree in the wood at the other side of the lake. And — and — ' I shivered at the memory of the six huge jaws snapping at the branch I'd been trapped on.

'So that's why they were so excited when they came back. They just wanted to play, I expect. You must be the first living thing they've seen since I got here.'

'You mean you called them from here? But they were on the other side of the lake!'

The Jamshid pulled a tiny silver tube from his tunic pocket. 'A whistle, I think you call it. Very high-pitched. These girls ...'

'Girls? You call these things girls?'

'Of course. They're quite harmless. And they can pick up the sound of this whistle from miles away: sorry, kilometres! You've gone metric on Earth, haven't you?'

'How on — How do you know that?'

'Because I used to be a Wise One!'

'Then you must be ...'

'Hymir!' The Jamshid bowed very politely. 'Welcome to my island.'

'Yes!' I cried. 'Then you're the one I'm looking for.'

'Looking for me? Why?'

'Because you're the only one who can help me get back to my own time and place.'

Hymir stared into space for moment, then

looked at me.

'I'd give one of the Magyans' apples to know what you're talking about.'

I couldn't stop myself saying, 'If it hadn't been for an apple, I wouldn't be here now.'

'Why not?' he said, and I told him the whole story.

'Interesting.!' Hymir said the word very slowly. 'So a Jamshid managed to get to Earth, did he? They must be getting careless.'

'Who are they?' I asked.

'My brother Wise Ones. And if they can make a mistake like that, one that enabled a Jamshid to escape, then the time would be right for me to seize power. To rule on my own. If only ...'

'Can you?' I cried.

'With the right things,' he said.

'No, I mean help me get home.'

Hymir gazed into the distance for a moment and then said, 'I could, I suppose. But if I do, there's something you have to do for me!'

'I'll do anything.'

'I think,' said Hymir, 'you'd better listen to what it is first before you make any rash promises!'

CHAPTER

10

'What do you mean, rash promises?'

'Well, I don't mean an IOU with chickenpox,' said Hymir. 'I mean before you say you'll do anything, you should stop and think what "anything" could mean.'

'What does it — er — mean?'

'I think, before I answer, you'd better come and dry yourself.'

I looked down at the pebbles and realized I'd been sitting in a large puddle formed by drips from my sodden clothes.

Now, as I stood up one of the three dogs that had been crouching a little way off, padded up and began to lick my face.

It would have been bad enough being licked by one sandpapery tongue. Being slavered over and licked by two flopping out of mouths both with a terminal case of bad breath gave me goosebumps all over.

'Leave him alone, Alecto,' said Hymir.

'Thanks,' I said as he held out a hand and pulled me to my feet.

He led me to a gap in the scrub. 'This way,' he said. 'Careful, though, these leaves are as sharp as razors!'

The sky had cleared completely, the suns were blazing down and it wasn't too long before sweat was running down my brow.

'Is it much further?' I panted, trying to catch my breath.

'Just round the next bend,' he said.

I followed him into a large clearing. In the middle was a hut about two, maybe three times as big as Dad's garden shed at home.

'There's an old tunic in there. In the wardrobe. Should fit you. Whoever was here before me must have left it behind.'

If what was inside the hut was anything to go by, Hymir must have been living very simply.

A bed was pushed against one wall and a wardrobe against another.

A table and one chair.

And that was it.

I took off my sodden clothes and looked around for a towel.

There was one hanging behind the door.

A few minutes later when I had dried off and put on the tunic, I went back outside, clutching my clothes.

'Put them there in the suns.' Hymir said. 'They'll soon dry.'

'Why do you live here?' I asked when I had laid my clothes out. 'Why are you not with the other —

other —'

'Convicts?' Hymir's voice was bitter. 'They wouldn't dare risk it.'

'They?'

'My brother Wise Ones!'

'Why not?' I asked.

'Because they know how popular I am. I'm not being boastful,' he said, 'just stating facts. And they know I'm the only one in the Underworld who knows how to get back up. So they sent me here.'

'Why can't you get back up from here?'

'There's an invisible shield round the edge of the crater,' he said. 'If I tried to get through it, I'd turn to stone.'

'Does that mean you'll never be able to get off the island?'

'It looked that way,' Hymir said, 'until you came along. Now? Who knows?'

There was something about the way he was looking at me I didn't like, didn't like at all.

'I'll do anything to help,' I cried. 'Just ask me.'

'For me to get through the barrier safely without turning to stone, I have to have three things with me. And you'll need something else if you're to get back to Earth.'

'If you know what the things are, why don't you get them?' It seemed an obvious question to me.

Hymir raised his eyes heavenward as if to say 'give me strength' just like Mum does when there's an odd number of socks in the wash — which is mostly.

'Because what I — and you — need is on the other side of the barrier.'

'If I get them for you, will you tell me how to

get home?'

'If I get them for you,' he repeated my words. 'Oh, Per, how easy you make it sound!'

'Why?' I said. 'What do I have to do?'

'If I tell you, you must promise to try to get them. There can be no going back.'

'I promise!'

'And if you do, I promise to help you get home, even though you'll meet someone who will make you think your worst nightmares are coming true.'

'It's a deal,' I cried, spitting on my hand and holding it out for Hymir to shake — just like I'd seen them do in cowboy films on television.

Hymir looked at my hand as if it were a piece of rotting fish.

'What do I have to get?' I asked, rubbing my hand on the bottom of my tunic.

'Oh, just the hair from a dead lion! A bird's egg. An apple — '

He stopped.

'Not your favourite fruit, I suppose.'

'You can say that again.'

He looked puzzled. 'Why? Why should I say that again?'

'It's an expression. On Earth. If someone says something that's an ... an ... ' I fumbled for the word. ' ... understatement, we say, "you can say that again!"'

'How very confusing.' Hymir shook his head.

'You said we needed four things!' I said, blinking to avoid the disbelieving look clouding his eyes. 'You've only mentioned three.'

'Oh, yes,' he said, nodding his head. 'The fourth. Ah, the fourth. A sunflower's head.'

'The hair from a dead lion!' I said, shrugging my shoulders. 'A bird's egg, an apple and a sunflower's head. Doesn't seem too bad.'

Hymir threw back his head and began to laugh. He roared with laughter until there were tears running down his snout.

'I've heard of crocodile tears,' I said to myself. 'And now I've seen alligator ones. Well, alligatory ones, I suppose!'

'Oh, Per! Per! Per!' he chortled. 'Doesn't seem too bad, you say.'

'Well, it doesn't!'

'You have to kill the lion,' he said, suddenly serious. 'The stympha bird whose egg you have to get could eat you for breakfast and would given half a chance. The apples are in an orchard owned by three Magyans and protected by a snake. And the sunflower's head is kept in a bag hanging from Agnantha's waist ...'

'Agnantha!'

'Dreadful woman,' Hymir said. 'Whoever or whatever looks her in the eye is instantly turned to glass!'

You could have heard me gulp if you were standing beside a Boeing 747 taking off.

'What weapons will I have?'

'Weapons? I have no weapons to give you.'

'Listen,' I said, 'can we talk about this?'

Hymir shook his head. 'You promised, Per!'

Me and my big mouth.

CHAPTER

And that's why, about a week later, Alecto and I were halfway up a hill following a trail of enormous footprints in the dust.

'Alecto?' did I hear you say?

Yes! Alecto.

For some reason the two-headed mutt had taken what Gran would have called a shine to me.

Wherever I went, the beast followed me. Whenever I sat down, it ambled up to me and licked me all over with one or other of its two tongues.

When I woke up in the morning on the makeshift bed Hymir had made out of some old sacks stuffed with leaves, guess what had crept into the hut during the night and plonked itself beside me, so that the first thing I saw, and smelt, when I opened my eyes was — Alecto.

'Why's it called Alecto?' I asked Hymir.

He looked at me curiously.

'Don't they teach you anything at school on Earth nowadays?'

It could have been Gran speaking. 'What on Earth do they teach you at school nowadays?' she used to say when I gave her the wrong change after she'd asked me to go to the supermarket for her.

'Alecto was one of the three Classical Furies — the goddesses of vengeance!'

'We've got a dog at home,' I said.

'What's it called?'

'Di!'

'Same thing, I suppose!' said Hymir.

I didn't ask what he meant.

Hymir spent most of the time telling me about the tasks that lay ahead. And the more I heard, the more I began to wish I'd kept my big mouth shut.

The lion, the birds, the apples and Agnantha all lived in various parts of the Jamshid Underworld where prisoners who had served their sentences were sent to live when they were released from the penal island.

'Does no one ever get back up?' I asked.

Hymir shook his head. 'Never! That was the way of the first Wise Ones, and it's been the way ever since.'

'How will I find where they all are — the lion and the others?' I asked.

Hymir rummaged in the back of the wardrobe and took out a sheet of paper which he unfolded.

'The lion is there,' he said, pointing to a range of mountains. 'And the stympha bird's nest is on these cliffs here.'

'High?'

'Very!' he nodded, pointing to a large green patch on the map. 'The orchard is in the middle of this meadow.'

'And Agnantha?'

'Agnantha! Agnantha! Agnantha! Let me see. Where will the old crone be at this time of year?' he wondered aloud, stroking the end of his leathery snout. 'She should be there, in her holiday home, I suppose!' he said, gesturing to an island in the middle of a small lake.

My dreams were filled with great big lions being pecked to death by enormous birds, with me tumbling from Granny Smith's apple tree right at the feet of PC Crosseye who changed into an ugly old witch the moment I touched the ground. When I reached up to try to grab the bag from around her waist, she had looked straight into my eyes and I was turned into a glass statue!

And when I woke, the sight of Alecto gazing slavishly at me with her four bloodshot eyes made me want to turn over and go back to my nightmares again.

'I think you'd better take her with you,' Hymir said, when I was getting ready to set off.

'That thing?' I pointed at the four-eyed cur.

'She could come in useful! And so will this,' he said, handing me what looked like a tiny Walkman earphone. 'Put it in your ear.'

Puzzled, I slipped it in.

'Can you hear me?' Hymir asked.

I nodded.

'And can you understand what I'm saying?'

'Sure!'

'Good. I'm speaking Jamshid.'

'Neat,' I thought, pulling it out and peering at it.

And that's why as I rowed away from the island, there was an evil-breathed dog slavering all over me, two more on the beach howling miserably at Hymir's feet and I had what Hymir called a Babelometer in my ear.

Not only would it make me understand whatever was said to me, he had explained, it would also make whatever I said understandable to anyone I talked to.

'I could do with that for maths,' I thought, remembering the look that appeared on Pongo's face whenever she asked me to explain something I should have learned for homework.

'If you do make it back, you'll find me at the hut,' Hymir had called as he waved me goodbye. The way he said 'if' had sent a shiver down my spine.

Hymir had said that when we reached the bottom of the mountains where the lion lived, I'd soon meet up with the Jamshids who lived there.

But there didn't seem to be any. Or if there were, they were keeping well out of sight.

We had started to make our way along a path that looked as if it led to the foothills when I spotted a rag fluttering from a thornbush.

'I know what that is, Alecto,' I said, pulling it off. 'It's part of a Jamshid's tunic.'

The dog turned one of her heads towards me and sniffed the cloth I was clutching.

'Go find,' I said, as if I was talking to Di.

Alecto sat on her haunches and sniffed the air all around.

One of her noses must have smelt something,

for when she stopped sniffing, she turned both heads in the same direction, sat down and thumped her great tail on the ground.

'Go get it!' I said.

Alecto ran like the wind into the scrub at the side of the path. A moment later I heard her bark nervously and then a bloodcurdling moan drifted towards me, a moan so full of despair that waves of fear began coursing through every vein in my body.

CHAPTER

12

I tore towards the sound. 'Down, girl' I cried. 'Down!' For the dog was on its hind legs, its front paws pinning a terrified Jamshid against a large boulder.

'Call her off,' he pleaded. 'Please!'

'Down, Alecto,' I commanded.

Alecto padded towards me, her tongues hanging out.

'Thanks,' said the Jamshid. 'Thought she was about to have my throat out.'

'No!' I smiled. 'She's as good as gold. Aren't you, girl?' I said, bending down to pat her on the back.

'You're not from these parts, are you?'

'Ten out of ten for observation,' I thought, and then said, 'No!' And before he could ask me where I came from, I went on. 'It's a long story and I don't really have time. I'm looking for a lion.'

The Jamshid's face went white. 'You're looking

for a lion?' he said as if he didn't believe what he'd just heard.

'That's right.'

'You don't mean Nemea, do you?'

'That's the one,' I said.

'B-b-b-b-ut no one goes looking for Nemea! No one in their right mind that is! He prowls around here all day, killing whoever he comes across and drags their bodies back to his lair. Why do you think we spend our lives in hiding.'

'So that's why there was no one around,' I said.

The Jamshid nodded. 'Why do you want to go looking for trouble?' he said.

'Don't ask.' I shook my head. 'I've just got to find him, that's all.'

'He lives in a cave in that hill there. The one at the base of the snow-capped mountains.' The Jamshid turned and pointed to a little rounded hill to my left.

'Thanks,' I said. 'Come on, Alecto!'

'Hang on,' said the Jamshid. 'You can't — I mean — he-he-he's vicious —He-he-he'll ...'

'I've got to risk it,' I said.

'Well, er, all I can say is Good Luck.'

He held out a claw for me to shake. 'Don't suppose I'll be seeing you again. No one who goes into the foothills has ever come out again. If you do, you'll be the first.'

I remembered something Gran had once said when I'd come third in the sack race on school sports day and had gone home bitterly disappointed. 'Being first isn't the most important thing in life!'

If she'd been standing in front of me now, I'd

have told her to eat her words.

☀

I think they call them 'foothills' because climbing them is so sore on your feet.

And your back.

And your legs.

But it was my feet that hurt most of all as we toiled up the hill.

Alecto loved it. She bounded ahead then stopped and waited with an expression on her faces that seemed to say, 'Come on. You are so slow!'

About halfway to the brow of the hill, the path forked.

'OK, which way?' I said to Alecto.

I hadn't been expecting an answer, of course, but I sort of got one.

Alecto sat at the fork, one head gazing up the left-hand fork, the other staring up the right-hand one.

I looked around for a twig. 'Heads we go to the right: tails to the left,' I said, spinning it round on a small rock in the path.

It came to rest pointing at Alecto's left eye.

'Heads it is,' I said. 'Come on, girl!'

I set off to the right. Alecto stayed where she was.

'Alecto! Here!' I clicked my fingers. 'Come on!'

My shout fell on deaf ears. Four deaf ears to be strictly accurate.

I walked back to where she was sitting.

'What's wrong?' I said, stroking her between

the ears of her left head.

The look she gave me reminded me of the one Cass, my sister, used to shoot my way if she had to go out and I forgot to record one of the soaps she's addicted to. 'Are you stupid or something?' she'd say and look at me in exactly the same way Alecto was gazing at me now.

'OK,' I sighed. 'We'll go to the left.'

As soon as I set off up the left-hand path, she was at my feet, tongues hanging out. 'Good girl,' I said.

The path wound this way and that through dense undergrowth until it widened into a clearing.

The path ahead was blocked by a rockface.

Large boulders made the way to the left impassable.

And the spiky bushes growing thickly on the right didn't look at all friendly.

Alecto, just ahead of me, stopped so suddenly that I tripped over her and landed painfully on something sharp.

It was only when I stood up that I realized what I'd fallen on.

My stomach churned when I found I'd been lying on a bone.

It heaved when I looked around and saw the whole clearing was littered with bones.

We seemed to have come to a dead end in every sense of the word!

Behind me, Alecto was sniffing the air and whimpering softly.

I turned round and saw her shy away from the rockface.

'What's wrong, girl?' I said, bending down to comfort her.

But before my hand had reached her ears, she shied away from me and shot into the undergrowth.

The almighty roar coming from within the crags had me right behind her before you could say 'Nemea'!

CHAPTER

13

When Hymir had said 'lion', I'd imagined something like the ones I'd seen at the Safari Park on the school outing last year.

I'd forgotten I was on another planet among aliens — and an alien's idea of a lion was not my idea of a lion!

The beast that padded out of a cave in the rock-face was the same, tawny colour as lions on Earth and had the same shaggy mane.

But no lion I'd seen before had two sabre-like teeth sticking out from either side of its mouth.

And no big cat had claws that looked like scythes curving upwards from its paws. With claws like that, you wouldn't need a food blender: these would turn a lump of steak into a pile of mince in a couple of slashes.

The great beast picked its way through the bones, prowling round the clearing as if it was looking for somewhere to bask in the warm sunshine.

I could feel Alecto quivering with fear beside me.

She could probably feel me quivering beside her.

As he slumped to the ground, Nemea yawned. From where I was crouching, I was staring into two lines of swords glinting in the sun.

I must have moved for I felt a sharp pain as something dug into my leg, just above my knee.

'Aagh!' I winced and looked round to see I'd brushed against the meanest-looking spiked leaf.

I tugged at it, hoping to free it. But the enormous spike had become embedded firmly in my flesh.

It was only when I started to tease it out, I realized the end was curved like a fishing hook, and had a little spike sticking out just where it curved.

As gently as I could, I twisted it round and, clenching my teeth to try and make the pain more bearable, I managed to get it out.

The leaf was so sharp and so big it reminded me of one of those enormous hooks you sometimes see in a butcher's shop with whole legs of meat hanging from them.

'Well, at least I've got a weapon now. In fact,' I thought, looking around me, 'I've got an undergrowth full of weapons.'

As quietly as possible, I began to break off as many spikes as I could from the bushes. Some were as straight as daggers, others hooked and curved.

Suddenly I heard something that for a moment made me think I was back home again, and everything that had happened to me had been a terrible nightmare.

Snoring.

I peered out at Nemea.

He was out cold, just like Gran on a Sunday afternoon after she had demolished everything that was put on her plate.

'That's far too much for me,' she'd say, eyeing the slices of meat Dad was piling onto her plate. 'Oh well, perhaps just one more. And maybe another potato. No, make that two!'

And once she'd settled in her armchair in front of the television, that was her gone. World War Three could have started in our back garden and she wouldn't have stirred.

I prayed that Nemea was just as sound a sleeper as I slithered on my belly through the under-growth, a dozen spikes in my left hand, my right hand empty.

I'd picked up a long bone and stuck it into the top of my jeans so that it ran up my back.

Every time I inched forward the top of that bone dug into the back of my head so hard it was all I could do to stop myself shouting with each jab.

It seemed I had been waiting for ever by the bushes, a few feet from Nemea, when I saw the slumbering beast's great jaws about to stretch wide open in another mammoth yawn.

I pulled the bone from my waistband and streaked forward at the speed of light.

OK, I'm exaggerating, but I've never moved quite so fast in my life before.

The beast woke just as its great jaws were at their widest.

Praying the bone was strong enough and

wouldn't splinter under the pressure, I rammed it into the awesome mouth, threw my arms round its neck and jerked myself onto its back, just as I'd seen cowboys do in TV Westerns.

Gripping as tightly as I could, I held onto the thick mane with one hand and stabbed over and over again with the spikes and hooks in my clenched fist.

The beast was in a frenzy.

It bucked like a wild horse.

It kicked out like a mule.

I could see the fearsome claws on its front feet lash out at Alecto who was frantically running round and round, mostly keeping well out of the way but every now and then seizing a chance to dart in to sink her teeth into the agonized lion's fleshy haunches.

I'd been on the Whiplash at the fair.

I'd been on the Big Dipper at one theme park.

And I'd been on the Roller Coaster at another.

Pieces of cake compared to what I was going through now.

I was being tossed about like a herring in a hurricane, but somehow I found the strength to hold on.

With blood oozing from hundreds of cuts, Nemea sank to the ground.

I don't know how I knew what it was going to do next, but I did.

Somehow I sensed it was going to roll over to trap me under its massive bulk.

At the last moment, I sprang forward, leapfrogged over its head and streaked for the undergrowth, turning as I ran to see the stricken beast, its jaws clamped open by the bone in its mouth, collapse in a pool of blood.

Alecto took one last lunge at the dying beast before slinking to my side.

'Well done, girl!' I was panting as fast as she was. 'Well done!'

We watched the lion close its eyes, as its lifeblood seeped away.

I was about to approach to pluck a handful of hair from its mane, when the eyes opened and stared into mine.

My blood turned to ice as the lion raised its head and let out a mighty roar.

Then, as if a red veil had been pulled over its now dull yellow eyes, they closed for the last time and Nemea's head slumped to the ground.

I picked up a bone and threw it at the great carcass — just to make sure.

No response.

I edged closer, my heart pounding like an express train, picked up another bone and prodded the mountain of flesh in front of me.

When I was quite certain it was dead, I forced myself forward the last few inches and pulled a clump of hair from its tangled mane.

One down. Three to go.

CHAPTER

14

Birds!

If these things circling high overhead were birds, then Santa Claus comes round on Hallowe'en.

Alecto and I had made our way through thick woodland to get to the cliffs where the stympha birds laid their eggs, and we were now standing at the bottom of crags so tall their tops were out of sight.

And whirling around up there was a flock of the meanest looking birds I've ever set eyes on.

Even at this distance, I could hear their great leathery wings flap against their plump, feathered bodies. And their beaks, as sharp and long as a knight-of-old's lance, caught the sun and shone like bronze.

As I gazed upwards, something swished through the air towards us.

The next thing I knew Alecto had knocked me

out of the way so violently I'd fallen on my back and rolled over to the right.

I was about to say 'Stupid dog' when something plunged into the ground just at the exact spot where I had been standing.

It quivered briefly and then was still.

'What the ... ' I gasped, stretching over to tug it out.

One end was feathered, like a dart, the bronze shaft tapered to a point as sharp as a needle.

As I lay there staring at it, another thudded into the ground a few inches to my left, then a third just to my right.

I looked up.

The birds had swooped down so low I could see that their wings were thickly fringed with these darts.

And as the birds swooped down again, it was obvious they were out for a spot of target practice: and who was the bull's eye?

Me!

'Come on,' I shouted to Alecto, struggling to my feet amid the shower of darts raining down on us. 'Let's get out of here!'

Alecto didn't need much persuasion. Much? She didn't need any persuasion at all.

We ran like the wind, not stopping till I was certain we were out of range.

'What now?' I panted. 'How can I get one of their eggs if I can't even get near the cliffs they nest on?'

I still had some of the spikes and hooks I'd used to kill the alien lion, but I doubted if even they were sharp or strong enough to pierce the feathered body of one of these aerial dart throwers.

I sat there asking myself the same three questions over and over again.

How could I get to the cliff face?

If I did, how could I get up to the line of enormous nests I could see sticking out from a ledge about forty metres above the ground?

And supposing I did make it and managed to steal an egg, how would I get back down?

The first two questions were answered as I was asking myself the third for the hundred and second time.

Suddenly I felt a great rush of wind above my head. I looked up and saw one pair of enormous claws bearing down on me and another hovering just above Alecto.

Strong though Alecto was, there was nothing she could do to stop the great bird digging its talons into her heavy shoulders and whisking her heavenward.

I didn't have time to scream 'Bring her back!' before I felt a searing pain in my shoulder.

The next moment I too was being lifted into the air.

Looking down between my feet, I saw the trees and bushes getting smaller and smaller as I was swept towards the cliffs.

'Don't drop me,' I screamed. 'Please, don't drop me.'

The sharp talons dug painfully into my flesh, but seeing the widening gap between my feet and the ground I was actually quite glad to be gripped by them even though they were like red-hot pokers sticking through my flesh.

We were speeding towards the cliffs so fast I thought we would slam into them. But just as I was bracing myself for the collision, we shot higher.

We were so close to the rockface, I could almost feel my nose scrape against it.

Suddenly we stopped going up.

I looked down.

We were hovering above a pile of branches and twigs laid out in a circle.

Alecto was sprawled in the middle of the enormous nest, a bewildered expression on the face she turned towards me. She was surrounded by a clutch of eggs shaped like small rugby balls.

A moment later, I was dropped beside her.

I was about to say, 'Now what?' when I heard a loud splintering sound behind me.

I looked round.

A small bright brass beak was breaking through the shell of one of the eggs.

I watched, hypnotized, as thin cracks appeared all over the shell before it shattered to reveal a tiny stympha bird.

It didn't stay tiny for long.

As I watched, it grew before my astonished eyes until it was as tall as a chicken. Its bright eyes peered around it then fixed on Alecto and me.

There was something about its expression I didn't like.

It seemed to be saying 'starters' and 'main course'.

✪

The hatchling waddled across the nest towards us

like a pigeon with murder on its mind.

First things first.

I quickly picked up one of the eggs just in case we ever got back to Hymir and stowed it in a pocket. I hoped it wouldn't hatch there!

Thank goodness Mum had bought these jeans for me to grow into. The pockets were deep and wide.

Even so the idea of a bronze-beaked bird pecking its way through the denim was not one I found appealing.

As I took my hand out of the pocket, it caught one of the spikes held dagger-like in my belt.

They might not have been much use against the nestling's mother, but as I grabbed one in each hand and began to flash them through the air, the beady-eyed baby was kept at bay.

As I moved towards it, I felt as if I was walking through syrup.

Glancing down, I saw the bottom of the nest seemed to be made of sticky silk.

Alecto was growling both her heads off as I bore down on the baby bird.

Suddenly I heard a cracking sound on my left.

Then another on my right.

Oh no! Two more eggs were about to hatch.

Moments later, I had one bright-eyed little monster in front of me, another on my right and a third on my left.

Worse, a loud squawking overheard told me Mummy bird wasn't far away.

Her three newly hatched young were closing in.

I felt like the swordsman in a book I'd once read as I stood there trying to fend off the monsters, jabbing here, jabbing there, jabbing spikes every-where.

Had Alecto's hair-raising growls been directed at me, I would have backed off right away: they had no effect at all on the evil-looking nestlings who were pecking at our feet.

Inch by inch we fell back, Alecto and I, away from the cliff face.

One moment, there was solid rock under the silky floor of the nest, the next, I felt as if I was walking on air.

We were on the part of the nest jutting out over the ledge.

'No!' I screamed as I felt it overbalance under our weight and start to topple.

With a chorus of pathetic squawks, the three baby birds shot over my shoulder as if they had been flipped by a tiddleywink, and plunged head first out of the nest.

'Me next,' I gulped, falling backwards into the void.

Desperate to find something to grab, anything to delay my fall, my arms flailed in all directions.

Just as I was about to go over the edge, I heard a loud yelp.

'Sorry, girl!' I was clutching Alecto's tail.

With a loud creak, the nest overturned com-pletely. As it went, a gnarled, branch that had been sticking out of the side, spun round and lodged itself right across the middle of the falling nest.

I closed my eyes, expecting to feel myself crash-ing to the ground.

But I didn't.

I was floating gently down like a feather.

Opening my eyes and gazing up, I saw that the most extraordinary thing had happened.

In her frantic scrambling to avoid falling over the cliff, Alecto had locked her jaws onto the knobbly branch, and as the nest overturned completely and started its descent, the silky bottom had billowed out like a parachute.

We were wafted gently to the ground, me holding on to Alecto's tail with both hands now, Alecto biting the branch.

As my feet touched the ground, I let myself fall backwards and rolled over a little, hoping to stop Alecto landing on top of me.

But I wasn't quick enough, and a moment later a tangled mass of dog and boy, both swathed in sticky silk, were writhing about trying to disentangle ourselves.

Breaking through the cocoon was like punching candy-floss.

But we did it and began fleeing from the cliffs, running as fast as we could.

The furious cawing of what sounded like a thousand birds and a hail of darts followed us.

'Keep going, Alecto,' I cried, knowing if we could make it to the woods, the trees grew too closely together for the birds to get to us.

I felt dart after dart pierce my neck, my back, my legs, but I raced on regardless.

I glanced round.

The flock was gaining on us.

'We're almost there,' I shouted.

Next thing I knew I was flying through the air, having tripped over something on the path, and I tumbled head over heels onto coarse grass.

I lay there, winded and bruised, knowing that
any second now I would be impaled on the end of
a brass beak as the leading bird swooped in for the
kill.

CHAPTER

15

I screamed as two sharp claws dug into my shoulder again.

I could do nothing to save myself. I waited to be whisked into the air and swept back to the nesting ledge, fodder for the newly hatched stympha birds.

But I wasn't.

Instead, I felt myself being dragged along the ground.

I managed to lift my head a little. Alecto had my jumper in her jaws and was tugging me towards the trees.

In a matter of moments we were there.

'Thanks, girl,' I panted, rising painfully to my feet.

I was wiping earth from my jeans and jumper when my hand brushed against a bulge in my pocket.

The egg! It must be in a million pieces.

But when I plunged my hand into my pocket,

there it was, intact, nestling in the clump of hair I'd torn from Nemea's mane.

'Nice and warm,' I said.

Warm! That was the last thing I wanted it to be. Birds sit on eggs to keep them warm so they hatch. I tore it from my pocket and held it at arm's length.

'Must cool it down,' I said aloud. 'It mustn't hatch. Water! We must find water.'

Alecto looked up at me then started to run through the trees.

She'd only gone about ten yards when she stopped, turned round and cocked her head as if to say, 'Come on then!'

I did my best to keep up with her as she romped through the woods, not pausing until we'd come to a stream. I remembered we'd passed it on our way to the cliffs.

Alecto lapped great mouthfuls of water as I plunged the egg over and over again into the ice-cold water. If the cold didn't kill the little stympha inside, surely the shaking would.

After about five minutes, I stopped. 'If that doesn't do it, nothing will,' I said.

With the dirt and strands of lion hair washed off it, the egg shone in my hand so brightly I could see my reflection in it.

'Come on, girl,' I said, playing with Alecto's ears. 'Time to go.'

The meadow where the Magyans' orchard lay, Hymir had said, was on the far side of the wood and almost as soon as we were out of the trees, I could see a hedged enclosure not far away.

'There it is,' I cried, pointing.

We walked towards it — well, I walked, Alecto

ran all over the place. The two suns blazed out of a clear sky.

I still thought it was funny, they cast not one, but two shadows. When Alecto was behind me, it was as if I was being followed by a four-headed monster.

As we neared the orchard I could see fruit trees above the top of the hedge.

They were laden with pears and plums, lemons and oranges.

Right in the middle and taller than all the others, its branches groaning with golden fruit, was the most magnificent apple tree I'd ever set eyes on.

The apples on Granny Smith's tree — including the one I'd been reaching for when Crosseye had caught me red-handed, the one that had got me into this mess — weren't half the size of these.

There was a gate in the hedge that swung open as soon as I touched it.

A curious, creepy stillness surrounded me as I cautiously edged into the orchard. Alecto, who till now had been panting like a steam train, also fell silent.

'Good morning!'

I almost jumped out of my skin as I spun round to see who had spoken.

'Over here!'

There, seated on a marble bench in a corner of the garden, were three of the most beautiful creatures I had ever seen.

The radiant emerald, almond-shaped eyes were so bright they cast a glow over their satin-smooth, brown skin.

They stood up and the long silver tunics they

wore reached down to the ground.

Alecto growled softly as they beckoned us towards them.

I saw the mouth of one move, but I couldn't understand the tinkling words that fell from her lips.

'Hang on,' I said. 'I think my Babelometer's gone on the blink!'

Despite Gran's warning about never sticking anything smaller than your elbow into your ear, I poked my index finger into my right ear and found the little earplug had come loose.

'Sorry, what did you say?'

Again the beautiful creature's lips moved. 'I said, welcome to our garden.'

If flowers could speak that's how they would sound.

'Thank you,' I said. 'You must be the Magyans!'

The tallest of the three nodded.

'Why have you come?' the second one asked.

'We don't get many visitors,' said the third.

'Especially curious-looking ones like you!' the first said.

'An a-p-p-ple!' I stammered. 'I need one of your a-p-p-ples!'

The tinkling laughter that greeted my words sounded like notes played on a crystal pipe.

'Help yourself.'

Alecto growled again.

'It's all right, girl,' I soothed her. 'They're nice and friendly. They said we can take an apple.'

But as I looked at them again, I saw their expressions change.

Their eyes narrowed into little more than slits.

Their mouths smiled cruelly, taunting me.

'Take as many as you want,' the words shot from the tallest one's mouth.

'If you can,' spat the second.

'The apple tree's right in the middle,' rasped the third.

'What's wrong?' I asked. 'A moment ago you were as friendly as could be. Now I could be your bitterest enemy, judging from the way you're talking.'

My question was answered by a heart-stopping hiss.

Oops! I'd forgotten about the snake! The one guarding the apple tree.

✪

With Alecto at my heels and the three Magyans behind her, I made my way to the middle of the orchard.

Coiled around the gnarled tree trunk was the glistening body of a plump snake. Its tail flicked the earth around the roots, then suddenly shot out towards me as if it was about to wrap itself round my ankles.

I fell back.

'Well, go on.' I recognized the voice of the tallest Magyan. 'Go and pluck your apple! We won't try to stop you.'

'We never do,' said the second. 'We can't.'

'Not that we have to,' laughed the third.

'What insolence,' snapped the first.

'Asking for one of OUR apples!' the others chorused.

The head of the fearful snake was hidden by leaves. I turned away to face the Magyans.

'Want to see its head?' asked the first Magyan.

I was about to say 'not really', but before I could, one of the others picked a handful of plums from an overhanging branch and walked towards the apple tree, holding them out in her cupped hands.

The leaves rustled wildly as the serpent's head appeared and it began to unwind the top of its body from the trunk.

There was a bulge below its mouth, like a cobra's, and its fangs flicked furiously as it reached down to take the plums into its gaping jaws.

'Loves them,' said one of the Magyans. 'But the plum tree's forbidden to him.'

'It will do anything for a plum,' said another. 'Absolutely anything at all!'

'Would it?' I said to myself, watching the juice dribbling out of the sides of the serpent's purple-smeared jaws. 'Would it indeed?'

I suddenly knew what to do.

I reached up and before the Magyans could stop me, pulled a fruit-laden branch from the plum tree.

Springing forward, I dangled it in front of the serpent's head, just out of reach.

As it twisted and stretched, desperate to reach the fruit, I started to move round and round the tree.

I felt like a maypole dancer getting farther and farther from the pole as I ran round and round moving away from the tree all the time.

When I saw its entire body had now uncoiled itself from the tree, I threw the branch deep into the orchard.

Saliva foaming round its mouth, the frenzied serpent shot after it.

I was up that tree in a flash and down again a second later, an apple in my hand.

Holding it up by the stalk, I dangled it in front of the Magyans' furious faces.

'Mine, I think,' I said.

And to the sound of the serpent pulping plums in its jaws, Alecto and I dashed for the gate.

'He did it,' I heard the first Magyan cry. 'He got one of our apples!'

We were almost at the gate when it slammed shut in our faces.

I tugged and tugged but it was stuck fast.

I spun round and saw the triumphant look on the Magyans' faces.

'No one leaves our orchard alive,' they screamed.

CHAPTER
16

That's what they thought!

As I spun back to tug at the gate again, I felt great clumps of earth hit my shins.

I looked down. Alecto was scraping frantically at the soft earth at the bottom of the gate.

If you ever need a trench dug at the speed of light, Alecto's the dog for you. She was under that gate in a flash, and I was hot on her tail.

As we ran across the meadow and back to the wood, I could hear the Magyans' anguished howls behind me.

They could scream all they liked: I had three of the things I needed.

Now for the fourth.

The sunflower head in the bag around Agnantha's waist.

The lake was beyond the far side of the wood, and it was getting dark when we reached it, too dark for us to try to puzzle out how to get to

Agnantha's island.

This would be our third night away from Hymir's hut.

We'd spent the first one in a clearing close to where I'd killed Nemea and the second in a cave we'd stumbled on in the wood.

'I'd love a proper bed tonight,' I said. 'And something filling to eat — a plateful of fish fingers and chips smothered in tomato sauce maybe. Or a deep pan pizza with extra pepperoni on the side.'

The nuts and berries Hymir had pointed out to me as safe to eat were OK, but they were nothing compared to a cheeseburger with great squidgy dollops of yellow oozing out of the bun. Nothing at all.

I sat on the banks of the lake, watching the water turn from deep purple to black as evening gave way to night and feeding Alecto some nuts I'd picked in the woods, I dreamt of a decent meal.

Suddenly Alecto jerked her heads away and sat bolt upright, sniffing the air.

So was I a second later when the mouth-watering smell of something cooking wafted through the air.

'Oooh,' I sighed, breathing it in.

Alecto whined.

'Come on, girl,' I said, clambering to my feet. 'Let's go and investigate.'

Alecto didn't need to be told twice. She was off like a shot.

The Jamshidian Underworld might have two suns, but it only had one moon. And it was bigger by far than ours and ten times as bright.

We ran along the banks of the lake until we

came to a dense clump of trees.

I stopped.

Alecto plunged straight in.

The loud, agonized scream I heard a second later had me casting my mind back to the day I first set eyes on Alecto.

'Get off!' a voice screamed. 'Call him off, someone. PLEASE!'

I ran through the trees shouting, 'Alecto! Good girl! Here girl!'

I crashed into a dimly lit clearing and saw Alecto on her hind legs, her paws pinning a plump Jamshid against the wall of a small wooden cabin.

'Down, girl,' I cried. 'Down!'

'Thanks,' the Jamshid gasped when Alecto was sitting calmly at my feet. 'Thanks a ...'

He stopped in mid-sentence and I could see him running his eyes all over me.

'What — who — are you? You're not a Jamshid!'

As quickly as I could I told him my story.

'Who?' the Jamshid stopped me when I mentioned Hymir. 'You know the Wise One?'

I nodded. 'Yes. And that's one of his dogs. He promised to help me return to my world if I got him the three things he needs to get back up.'

'Hymir's planning to go back up?' the Jamshid's eyes widened. 'I'd do anything to help him. I'm Eryman, by the way,' he went on, holding out a claw for me to shake.

'If Hymir was the Wise One in charge, things would be a whole lot better, I can tell you,' Eryman said. 'These tyrants running things now send anyone who disagrees with them about anything down here, no matter how trivial it is. How do you think I ended up down here?'

I shrugged my shoulders. 'I've got three of the things he told me to get. One more to go.'

'What's that?'

'A sunflower head. Someone called Agnantha has it in a bag tied to her waist.'

'Agnantha!' Eryman was horror struck. 'You'll never do it.'

I took the three things out of my pocket. 'I killed a lion to get this hair,' I said, holding up the clump of Nemea's mane for him to see. 'And I was almost killed by cannibal birds getting this egg.'

'You'll be telling me next that the apple comes from the Magyans' orchard.'

I nodded.

'You mean you killed Nemea, got a stympha's egg and a Magyan apple?' He fell back in astonishment. 'Well I never,' he whispered. 'Well I never!'

'How can I get to the island?' I asked. 'To find Agnantha?'

'You know what happens to anyone she sees looking her in the face?' Eryman said. 'They're turned to glass.'

'I know. But I've got to try. Otherwise I'll be stuck here for ever.'

'It's too late to go there now,' said Eryman. 'You'd better come in and eat. I've just made some soup.'

'We smelt it,' I said.

'And once we've eaten, you can spend the night here. You must be exhausted.'

'You can say that again.'

'If you insist! You must be exhausted.'

✪

93

'There she is.' Eryman spoke in a whisper. 'Don't let the old witch see you.'

Eryman had rowed Alecto and me across the lake to Agnantha's island and we were kneeling behind bushes a few feet from where Agnantha was sitting.

'Don't worry, I won't,' I said. If I needed a reminder of what the old crone could do with her gaze, there was a menagerie of curious creatures of all shapes and sizes strewn around. All were made of glass.

Agnantha actually looked like my idea of a witch. Her face was covered in boils. Her long nose came to a sharp point and her little mouth, shaped like a slice of shrivelled lemon, hung open to reveal stumpy, blackened, uneven teeth.

Hymir and Eryman had both told me what would happen if she caught anyone looking directly at her. No one had mentioned that she only had one eye: a huge single, unblinking eye set right in the middle of her brow.

Alecto pawed the ground and rubbed her heads against her shoulders, desperately trying to dislodge the blindfolds I'd tied over her eyes to prevent her being caught in Agnantha's glassy stare.

'Look,' I whispered. 'There's the pouch! Hanging from a rope round her waist.'

'How are you going to get it?' Eryman breathed.

I'd spent all night puzzling over that one and still hadn't come up with an answer.

'I have to think,' I said.

'Who's there?' Agnantha's high-pitched, quavery voice grated on my ears. 'I know someone's there. Come out! Come out! Let me see you.'

We froze.

At least Eryman and I did.

Not Alecto. She growled, stood up, the hair on her back rising and sniffed the air.

'Come back, Alecto!' I cried as the huge dog leapt forward and bounded towards the old hag.

'Aaagh!' Agnantha's scream would have curdled milk as Alecto threw herself at her, knocking her off her chair and sending her sprawling to the ground.

I watched her wrinkled old hands flash upwards trying to tear the blindfolds from her assailant's eyes.

'Alecto!' I cried, crashing through the bushes, making sure I didn't look at the struggling crone.

The dog spun round and ran towards me, the loosened blindfolds falling from her eyes.

'Help me up,' screamed Agnantha, 'I can't move! Help me up and I promise not to turn you to glass.'

'Don't listen to her,' cried Eryman.

I could see the Jamshid, his hands over his eyes, reflected in the dog's four eyes and suddenly I knew how to come close enough to Agnantha to get the sunflower from the bag without risking looking directly into her blazing eye.

'Call her, Eryman,' I shouted, turning round so that my back was towards the stricken old witch.

'Eryman!' yelled Eryman.

'I didn't mean call her "Eryman", I meant call the dog!'

'Oh, sorry!' he roared. 'Here, girl! Alecto, come to Eryman.'

'Go to him, girl,' I screamed, desperately fumbling in my pocket for the stympha's egg.

Holding it just in front of my eyes, and a little to the right, I could see Agnantha reflected in it quite clearly.

I edged my way backwards and when I was almost by her side, knelt down.

I reached behind me and felt for the bag.

'Yes!' I cried, when I had it in my grasp. But as I struggled to tug it free, Agnantha's ice-cold fingers clamped round my wrist, holding me in their iron grip.

CHAPTER

17

I plunged the egg back in my pocket and pulled a spike from my belt.

'Take that!' I yelled as I stabbed it into the hand gripping my wrist. 'And that!'

Again and again I rammed the spike into the bony hand until I felt it relax and I was able to wrench my wrist free,

A final tug tore the bag from the rope, and I was off.

'Come on,' I yelled, streaking past Eryman and Alecto. 'Let's get out of here.'

We tore down to the beach and splashed through the water into Eryman's little boat.

Eryman grabbed the oars.

Alecto and I sat facing the island. 'Close your eyes,' Eryman cried, 'and don't open them again until we're back on the mainland.'

The dog, sitting at my feet, didn't object as I covered all her eyes with my hands, and with

Agnantha's cries rising above over the splashing of the oars we left the island behind.

I pictured the old hag standing on the beach willing us to open our eyes so that we could join her glass menagerie.

'It's OK,' Eryman said. 'You can open them now. We're well out of her range by now.'

Even so, I kept my hands clasped over the dog's eyes, and kept mine firmly shut until I heard the boat scrape against the bottom of the lake and I knew we were nearing the mainland.

'Where to now?' Eryman asked after he had tied up the boat and we were back in his hut.

'Back to Hymir,' I said. 'As soon as possible!'

'Know how to get there?'

'Sure! Coming with us?'

'Can't,' he said sadly. 'I can't leave here. Ever. Well, not as long as those three are running things up there.' He jerked his head upwards.

'How could they find out? If you left?'

Eryman held out his wrist and pointed a claw at a tiny red disc embedded in the leathery flesh. 'That!' he said. 'It sends out a signal that tells whoever's on tagging duty exactly where I am.'

'Exactly?' I said.

'Yes!' he nodded. 'They'll even know I've been to Agnantha's island. But you tell Hymir if he ever does get back up and takes over, to remember old Eryman and how he helped you get the sunflower head.'

'Of course I will,' I said. 'Promise!'

I was just about to leave when I saw Alecto's ears prick up.

'What is it, girl?' I asked as she started to growl

softly.

Eryman ran to the window. 'Jamshid troops! What in the name of the Gorkman can they want here?'

○

'Hide!' he snapped. 'They may be looking for you.'

'Where?' I whispered, looking around the bare little room.

'Up there!' He was pointing to a flight of flimsy wooden stairs. 'In the attic. And when you're up, pull the rope.'

'What about Alecto?'

'Leave that to me. Now, quickly. Go!'

Grabbing Agnantha's bag which now held my four prizes, I flashed up the stairs and tugged on the rope. With a soft creaking the staircase slid up into the attic, covering the hatch I'd squeezed through.

Almost immediately there was a loud knocking on the hut door.

'Come in!' Eryman called.

There was a tiny slit in the wooden planks I was lying on. Peering through it I saw three Jamshids, the feathers on their grey capes fluttering in the draught.

'You seen this thing?' asked one of them, thrusting a piece of paper into Eryman's claws.

Eryman shook his head. 'What is it?'

'A boy from the planet Earth. The form taken by the outlaw, Loki, when he escaped.'

'You mean there's life on Earth?'

The Jamshid nodded.

'And that's what they look like?'

'Yes!'

'What's he done? Why are you looking for him?'

'He was meant to be in the penal place, but when we did a snap count of the prisoners he was missing. Vanor, the captain of the prison ship, said he handed him over to Swingo ...'

'Old Swingo?' said Eryman. 'Is he still running the glince mine?'

The Jamshid nodded.

'Loki wouldn't be much good down the mines, not looking like that. Scrawny looking thing, isn't he?'

Scrawny! Me? Scrawny?

'Swingo said he used him as a messenger. To run here and there. And he scarpered.'

'Well, he didn't run here.'

'Sure?'

Eryman nodded. 'Haven't seen him. If I do ...'

Alecto's growl cut him short.

The Jamshid spun round. 'Where did you get that dog?'

Eryman bent down and stroked Alecto's ears. 'I was on the beach this morning when it appeared from nowhere and started to swim towards the island. Had to try to stop it. I mean, you know what happens to anything who looks Agnantha in the eye.'

'So that's why you went to the island?' the Jamshid said.

I saw Eryman nod his head.

'Very well. Right, you two, back to the trackjip!'

'Where did you park it?' asked Eryman.

'Other side of the clearing!'

The three Jamshids were just about to leave when Eryman said, 'You don't suppose he could be on the island, do you? The Earth child?'

'There's no way I'm going over there.'

'You don't have to look at her if you should stumble across her, you know.'

The Jamshid grunted.

'All you need is this mirror.' Eryman held one out. 'Walk backwards and hold it above your head. That way you'll be able to see her without looking directly into her eyes. And you'll be able to scout the island for the Earth boy. Take my boat if you want.'

The Jamshid took the mirror and held it above his head. 'See what you mean,' he said. 'Come on, men.'

I waited until Eryman called me to come down.

'There's a trackjip on the other side of the clearing,' he said.

'I know that!' I nodded. 'I was listening. But what's a trackjip?'

'A powerful motor. Travels over the roughest ground. Hundred times quicker than walking. You'll be back at Hymir's in hours rather than days. They're easy to drive. Press the red button to start the engine.'

'We'll be off then!'

'Bye!'

'Bye, and thanks for everything.'

A few minutes later, I was on the other side of the clearing looking at the most curious machine I'd ever seen.

Instead of tyres it had large red balls, three on

either side.

Stretched between them was a sheet of strong rubber.

Under it I could see parts of an engine and above the two balls at one end, there was a steering wheel with a bright red button in the middle.

'Come on, girl,' I said, jumping aboard.

No sooner had Alecto leapt up beside me than I heard the sound of twigs snapping underfoot.

I peered into the trees.

'You there! Loki! Get off the trackjip.'

I recognized that voice. It was the Jamshid who had spoken to Eryman.

I slammed my fist into the red button.

Nothing!

I punched it again.

The engine was as dead as a dodo.

CHAPTER
18

'Come on!' I pleaded, pressing the red button again and again.

The Jamshid was lumbering towards me when, wheezing like a bad case of bronchitis, the engine spluttered into life.

'Yes!' I cried as the trackjip began to roll forward, but when I looked behind me, the Jamshid already had a claw on the sheet at the back.

'Where's the accelerator?' I yelled.

The only thing I could see was a little lever sticking out of the side of the steering wheel.

I jerked it towards me and the trackjip shot backwards.

'Sorry!' I shouted, hearing the agonized cry of the Jamshid I'd just run over.

I pushed the lever away from me. The engine roared and we leapt forward so suddenly that only the fact that I was clutching the steering wheel stopped me being hurled off the thing.

Alecto was sitting beside me one second, the next she was rolling backwards, barking madly.

'Steady girl,' I shouted. 'We're off.'

'Loki!' The Jamshid bawled. 'Come back!'

I glanced over my shoulder. The Jamshid had struggled to his feet and was standing shrouded in dust, shaking his claws at me.

The countryside flashed by as we zoomed across the meadow where the Magyan orchard lay, roared round the wood and raced past the cliff where the stympha birds nested.

Alecto, bouncing about like a baby in a buggy, managed a growl as she recognized the spot where I'd killed Nemea.

'Its all right, girl,' I shouted to make my voice heard above the whining engine. 'We're almost there.'

She barked loudly when, a little later, the lake where Hymir had his island came into view.

'Brakes!' I wondered aloud as we sped towards it. 'Where are the brakes?'

There were none.

There was only one thing for it.

'Hang onto your hat, girl,' I shouted, pulling on the lever I had until then been pushing as far forward as it would go.

The trackjip's engine screamed in protest as it came to a shuddering halt and then ricocheted backwards, sending Alecto and me flying through the air like human — well, one human, one doggy — cannonballs.

We splashed into the water, throwing up more spray than a school of drunken dolphins.

No sooner had I come up, gasping for breath,

than I heard a loud explosion from the shore. Moments later a steering wheel and a burnt bit of rubber splashed into the water a few feet from me.

I looked behind me and saw the smoking wreck of the trackjip blackening the tree it had crashed into.

'Oh well,' I thought. 'I've still got six years before I can sit my driving test — if I ever get home. Plenty of time to learn how to come to a smooth stop and park properly.'

I heard Alecto's spluttering a few seconds before I saw her heads bobbing around in the water a few feet away. I swam towards her and put my arms around her necks.

Almost at once, I felt her great body rise in the water and I found myself sprawled across her back.

'Home, James, and don't spare the horses,' I said, remembering what Gran always said to Dad as he drove her home when she woke up after sleeping off her Sunday dinner.

And clutching on to Alecto's soaking coat, I was dog-paddled across to the island.

✪

'So you gave up, did you?' Hymir said sadly.
'No!'
'Then how did you get back so quickly?'
'I sort of stole a trackjip.'
'A what?'
'A trackjip. It's a kind of mobile bedstead!'
'I know exactly what it is.'
'Do you know what this is?' I asked, pulling the

damp clump of mane from Agnantha's bag.

'I don't believe it,' gasped Hymir. 'It's some of Nemea's hair.'

'And this?'

'It can't be. It is,' he whooped. 'It's a stympha's egg.' He took it from my hand and was gazing at it in amazement as I took the Magyans' apple out of the bag.

'Here, catch,' I said.

For a moment I thought he was going to drop the egg and let it crash to the floor. But he managed to juggle it in the air and caught the apple with one hand and the falling egg with the other.

'Hercules himself couldn't have done better,' he cried, and for an embarrassing second I thought he was going to hug me.

I don't know about you, but hugging is not on my list of one hundred favourite things.

I knew all about Hercules. He was a Greek guy who was given lots of tasks to do by some king or other.

'With these three things I can plan my escape from here.' Hymir's voice was triumphant as he jumped up and down with excitement.

'Hello! Remember me!' I said, waving my hand at him.

'Of course. Of course,' he said. 'But to help you I need ...'

'This?' I drew the sunflower head from the bag.

'You got Agnantha's sunflower from her waist? Why, only someone who knew how the Greek hero Perseus used his shield as a mirror ...'

I knew about Perseus too. Warned that he'd be turned to stone if he looked directly at the face of an old witch called Medusa, he used his shield as a mirror to avoid her gaze when he cut her head off. Where do you think I got the idea of looking at her reflection in the egg from?

I also knew that Hymir was busy putting two and two together and was about to come up with four.

'Per Dawson!' he mused. 'Per? It wouldn't be short for ...'

'Tell a soul and I'll smash the stympha's egg,' I shouted, making a grab for it.

'I won't, I won't, I promise,' he cried.

'Now!' I said. 'How do I use the sunflower head to get back to my own time and place?'

'Not far from here,' he said, 'there's a short, round pole. Set on top of it is a clockface. Not an ordinary clockface. It tells you the year, the month, the day of the week as well as the time. Reset it precisely to the time you want to return to Earth. Start with the year at the far left and work your way along through month, week, day and hour. Think you can do that?'

I nodded.

'Then put the sunflower head on the clockface and when the pole's two shadows make a perfectly straight line, you will be back on Earth on the exact date and at the time you've set.'

'Where is this pole?'

'Come outside and I'll show you.'

I followed him to the shingle beach.

'See that fell there?' He was pointing to a small, rounded hill just on the other side of the lake. 'It's right at the ...'

The rest of what he was saying was drowned

out by the noise of engines roaring across the lake.

'What's that?' I bawled to make myself heard.

'Jamshids!' Hymir shouted. 'They must have had a tracker device on the trackjip you stole!'

CHAPTER

'Hymir!'

Whoever was shouting was obviously using a megaphone or something, for he sounded like Pongo on school sports day when she was trying to round up the contestants for the sack race.

'What do you want?' Hymir bellowed.

'Loki! He is there with you.'

'No, he's not. Loki's still on Earth. I have Per Dawson with me. He was beamed to Jamshidia by mistake.'

'We're going to come ashore. Don't try to stop us.'

'I wouldn't be so stupid,' Hymir shouted.

He turned and ran back to the hut and came back a few moments later clutching the three trophies I had brought him.

By the time the boat was in the shallow water at the edge of the lake, we were standing, Hymir and I, behind Alecto and her two sisters, all growling threateningly.

'That's him! That's Loki,' said the leading Jamshid as he waded to the beach. 'Get these dogs out of the way.'

As the Jamshid spoke, Hymir held the shank of Nemea's mane high above his head.

The Jamshid stopped in his tracks.

'What's that?' he gasped. 'It looks like ...'

'Nemea's hair?' said Hymir. 'Correct!'

The Jamshid fell back.

'And I've also got this! And this!' Hymir held up the stympha's egg and the Magyans' apple.

'But with these you can breach the invisible barrier without turning to stone, and g-g-get back up.'

Hymir nodded.

The three Jamshids who were standing in the water clambered onto the beach and one by one dropped to their knees.

'We'll support you,' one of them said. 'Everyone will. Linus, Phimarus and Argo are becoming more and more unpopular with each day that passes. They've become little better than tyrants. All of Jamshidia will rally to your side.'

'Get off your knees,' Hymir said quietly, 'and come into my hut. There's a lot I have to know.'

'Do I have to come, too?' I asked. 'If it's all the same to you, I'd rather be on my way.'

'Of course, you would!' said Hymir. 'You know what to do?'

I nodded.

'You really aren't Loki?' one of the Jamshids asked.

'No, he's not,' Hymir answered for me. 'He's Pers — Per Dawson. And he wants to go home. He knows how.'

'You'd better take this then,' said the leading Jamshid, plucking a green feather from his cloak. 'The place is swarming with other agents all looking for you. If you stumble across any of them, show them this feather and say that Danaus has given you permission to go wherever you want.'

'Thanks,' I said, putting the feather in my pocket where it nestled beside Agnantha's sunflower head.

I bent down to stroke Alecto who was sitting with her tongues hanging out at my feet.

'Goodbye, girl,' I said. 'I'm going to miss you.'

Alecto stretched her neck and licked all over my face with her rough, wet tongues.

'I'll get one of my men to row you to the other side,' said Danaus, clicking his claws and pointing to one of the other Jamshids. 'Cretes. You, please.'

Hymir was at my side as I walked to the boat. 'Do you remember what I told you shortly after we met?' he asked.

'Which particular part?'

'About meeting someone who'll make you think your worst nightmares have come true.'

So much had happened that I had no recollection of Hymir saying anything about nightmares.

'Sorry,' I said. 'What about it?'

'Just that,' Hymir said. 'That somewhere on the hill you're certain to meet someone who'll make you think your worst nightmares are coming true.'

'How do I beat him?'

'I can't tell you that. Just remember my words.'

We were at the water's edge by now.

'I'll be off then,' I said, jumping into the boat.

'Thanks for telling me how to get home.'

'Thank you for getting me the things I need,' said Hymir. 'If there was anything else I could do, I would. To thank you.'

'There's the Jamshid called Eryman who helped me. He doesn't really deserve to be here.'

'Few do, if what I gather is correct. But if I do get back up and take over, Eryman will be one of the first to be allowed to go home.'

'Thanks!'

I paddled out to the boat and clambered aboard.

As soon as I was safely in, Cretes started to work the oars. The sight of him pulling them through the water reminded me of my voyage to the penal island.

'There is something else you could do,' I shouted to Hymir.

'What?' he called back.

'When you're in charge, there's another Jamshid, Clam, you could pardon. I liked him!'

'Clam the con artist?' Hymir laughed. 'Is that old rogue still alive? Consider it done.'

I remembered something else from that voyage.

'And if you really want to thank me,' I yelled, 'you could make Alkanvaald hunting compulsory.'

✪

The suns were shining brightly when I reached the bottom of the hill which was encircled by a fence, twice, maybe three times taller than me.

I walked right round it looking for a gate or a door or a gap I could squeeze through.

Was there one?

In a word: No!

'Oh, well,' I said to myself. 'Nothing for it. Just have to try to climb it.'

I ran round it again, scanning it for any gnarled bits I could grab on to, or holes I could use for finger and toe holds.

About halfway round, I spotted a section where the planks didn't quite meet and I began to climb.

The gaps were OK for my feet, but every time I put a hand into one, the wood splintered and pierced it.

I was determined to get over that stockade, so I kept going despite the pain.

I was concentrating so hard that I didn't hear anyone creep up on me!

I was about six feet off the ground when I felt something clamp on to my ankle.

Looking down I found myself staring into gaping Jamshid jaws.

One tug and I plunged to the ground.

Now I was eyeballing his great dinosaur-like feet.

'Got you, Loki!' he said.

'Hang on,' I cried, fumbling in my pocket for the feather I'd been given. 'I'm not Loki! Danaus said that if I met any Jamshids I was to show them this and say that I could go anywhere I wanted.'

The Jamshid took the feather from me and peered at it. 'It's Danaus's all right. You must have stolen it from him.'

'Come on!' I said. 'I'm only little. If you were my size would you try to pluck a feather from something Danaus's size?'

The Jamshid looked me up and down. 'Suppose

not,' he said, handing back the feather. 'But if you can go anywhere in the Underworld, why are you trying to get in there?'

'I have to,' I cried. 'It's the only way I can get home — to where I come from.'

'Better you than me,' said the Jamshid. 'Better you than me.'

'Can you give me a - sort of leg up? If you know what I mean?'

The Jamshid knelt down and held his claws together, and when I was balanced on them, pushed me up as far as he could.

Reaching up to my full height and stretching my arms until they felt as if they would shoot from my armpits, I managed to curl my fingers round the top plank and pull myself up until I was perched there, my legs dangling over the other side.

'Thanks,' I shouted down to the Jamshid.

'Don't mention it,' he waved. 'And good luck. If anyone's going to need it, you are.'

CHAPTER

20

The hill wasn't very high — a hundred, maybe a hundred-and-fifty feet.

Even from where I was standing at the bottom, I could see the pole at the summit.

'Soon be home,' I said. 'Won't be long now.'

All the way up I kept looking around me, expecting to see whoever Hymir had warned me about, but there was no one.

I clambered up to the top, took the sunflower head from my pocket and laid it on the ground.

The flat clockface was set into the top of the pole beneath a hinged cover. When I flipped it open I heard the soft whirring of wheels turning slowly.

There were four wheels for the year, two for the month, one for the day of the week and so on.

'Wow!' I thought to myself, 'I could set this to any time I wanted, go back to when I was a little kid and start all over again: or I could make it so I was eighteen or nineteen and finished with school.'

My fingers lingered over the wheels for a moment as I fought the temptation to make myself older or younger.

'No! I'll go back to my own time and place.'

I set the year, month and date. 'What time was it when I bumped into Loki?' I asked myself and then remembered it had been after school and the church bell was striking four.

Four o'clock: 16.00 hours.

Hang on!

If I set it at four o'clock, I might get back at the precise moment I crashed into Loki and find myself beamed up again.

'It would be a nightmare if that happened,' I said aloud.

'Need any help?'

I spun round.

'Who are you?' I gasped, for I hadn't heard anyone approach.

'Geryon! You must have heard of me.'

There was something in the way he spoke I didn't like. Something sinister.

'Hymir warned me that I would m-m-m-eet someone who would m-m-m-ake m-m-m-y nightm-m-mares come true,' I stammered.

Geryon threw his head back and started to laugh.

Cackle would be a better word. Peal after peal of mocking laughter rang in my ear.

'He was right!' snorted Geryon.

As he spoke, a great shadow passed over one of the suns.

I looked up and saw a flock of Alkanvaalds

circling in the air overhead.

A second later I was surrounded by them.

Desperately I tried to fend them off, but no sooner had I beaten one off than another dived in, beak first.

'Help me,' I screamed. 'Get them off.'

I was punching, kicking, but it was no good.

Wave after wave of the birds came in for the attack.

I fell to the ground and covered my face.

'This is it,' I thought. 'My worst nightmare.'

I felt the ghastly birds peck me all over.

And then the pecking stopped.

I opened my fingers a little, just in time to see one of the Alkanvaalds pick up the sunflower in his beak.

I struggled to get to my feet. 'Bring it back,' I screamed. 'Bring it back.'

But the bird took to the air and circled above me just out of reach.

'You'll never get back now,' mocked Geryon.

'He's done it!' I thought. 'He's made my worst nightmare ...'

Suddenly, Hymir's exact words flashed through my mind. '... somewhere on the hill you're certain to meet someone who'll make you think your worst nightmares are coming true.'

With that, I realized that what had just happened had all been in my mind. I'd been imagining it.

I closed my eyes, clenched my fists and pressed my knuckles together.

'This isn't happening,' I shouted aloud. 'This is only happening in my head.'

I opened my eyes. Geryon was still there. But the malicious grin had been wiped from his face and replaced by a look of utter astonishment.

'How did you ...' he began.

'I understood Hymir's warning,' I said, looking round me.

The sunflower head was still on the ground where I had put it.

'And just in time, too,' I added, for the two suns were almost exactly opposite each other in the sky and the shadows cast by the pole were about to form a completely straight line.

Geryon didn't try to stop me as I darted forward and picked up the sunflower head.

Now that I understood his trickery, he was powerless over me.

I spun the last wheels, setting the time at just before four o'clock in the afternoon, closed the lid and placed the flower on top.

At that exact moment the suns reached the point where the shadows cast by the pole made a dead straight line ...

★

I was flying down the lane.

'Per Dawson, you come back here!' PC Crosseye was hot on my heels.

Suddenly I realized there was someone blocking my path.

I skidded to a halt just in front of him.

'Got you!' I felt Crosseye's hand on my shoulder. 'And I've got a witness who ...'

He stopped in mid-sentence as the church clock started to strike four.